Shifter Chronicles

COYOTE'S KISS

CRISSY SMITH

Coyote's Kiss
ISBN # 978-1-78430-692-2
©Copyright Crissy Smith 2015
Cover Art by Posh Gosh ©Copyright July 2015
Interior text design by Claire Siemaszkiewicz
Totally Bound Publishing

Published in 2015 by Totally Bound Publishing, Newland House, The Point, Weaver Road, Lincoln, LN6 3QN, United Kingdom.

Totally Bound Publishing is a subsidiary of Totally Entwined Group Limited.

Totally Bound Publishing books by Crissy Smith:

Seduced by the Neighbour
Lacey's Seduction
Eternal
Bid High
Fated Love
Vamps in the City

Were Chronicles Volume One
Pack Alpha
Pack Enforcer
Pack Territory

Were Chronicles Volume Two
Pack Rogue
Pack Community
Pack Mates

Were Chronicles Volume Three
Pack Daughter
Pack Hunter
Pack Council

Were Chronicles Volume Four
Pack Security
Pack Beta
Pack Secrets

Corporate Wolves
The Favour
Losing Control

Secrets
The Shifter and the Dreamer

Shifter Chronicles
Birds of Prey
Bear Claw
Eye of the Tiger
Coyote's Kiss

COYOTE'S KISS

Dedication

This story is in loving dedication to my fur baby Taz.
He might not be with us any longer but he will always
be in our hearts. RIP, my little man.

Chapter One

Luca Perez grinned behind his mask as he heard Jamie Ward curse. A billow of smoke and ash rose from the training field, making the clear blue day seem drab and dreary.

"Damn it, Perez!" Jamie's growl could be heard across their headsets.

The big tough Coalition agent probably hadn't expected Luca to detonate the charge with Jamie's team still so close to the site. Luca was an expert, though, and he knew when and how to make an explosion. His years with the ATF had been productive. Not only did he specialise in undercover work, but he also knew how to make and disarm all types of bomb.

Today's exercise was supposed to help Luca and his partner Abilene Fox, along with the Coalition teams, bond and learn to work as a team. Luca had been excited when it had finally been his turn in the four-week series of drills to show off what he could do.

"That wasn't nice." Abilene bumped his shoulder as she crouched next to him.

Luca laughed before glancing at her. She was trying, he knew, but her lips twitched as she attempted not to join him in amusement.

"Oh come on," he teased.

"You're lucky it's not Zak on that side," she said.

She was correct. Zak Lewis wouldn't hesitate to beat Luca's ass. Of course then the strong tiger shifter would help him up. He'd become good friends with Zak when they'd both been undercover trying to take down a group of shifters that wanted to start a human and shifter war. Neither he nor Zak had known that the other was an agent but they'd formed a tight bond. Zak had saved his life so he would be forever grateful. Still, that wasn't the only reason he kept his pranks away from Zak. He didn't want Abilene to kill him.

His partner was fierce when someone she loved was in danger. She'd been seeing Zak for a month and already there was no doubt that they were in love. She spent almost every night with him, although she insisted that she and Zak didn't live together. Abilene paid her half of the rent for the apartment Luca and she had leased while on loan to the Coalition. However, he still went home to an empty place night after night.

"You better run, little coyote," Jamie's voice broke through his conversation, capturing his attention.

"You have to find me first, you big dumb bear," Luca taunted. They had to press the button to turn on the mic to talk to each other, and by keeping Jamie busy verbally sparring with him, Luca could take advantage and really mess with the Coalition.

Jamie growled again.

"Stop antagonizing him," Abilene whispered.

He just shook his head. Jamie's team was too far away to find where he and Abilene were holed up.

He'd run these kind of training missions before with the ATF, but working with the Shifter Coalition was different. When Luca was attempting to educate humans, he could afford to be a little lax on the trail he left behind when moving during the mission. With the Coalition his job was more difficult. Since every member in the teams was some sort of shifter they could use their superior senses to discover where he and Abilene were hiding.

"Oh, I'll find you," Jamie promised.

A screech came over the mic.

"Shit! Cody's team is shifting," Abilene cried, grabbing at his arm.

Luca was prepared for that, though. Cody Johnson ran the birds of prey unit. The dark canopy over his and Abilene's heads blended in perfectly so that even from the air they wouldn't be seen. "Just don't move around. We'll be good."

She huffed, causing him to bite back another laugh. There were four squads searching for him and his partner but Luca was certain he'd be the victor of this round. "Where's Zak?" he asked Abilene.

"He's coming up on the north side of the field," Abilene answered quietly. "But they aren't on our path." She lowered her binoculars.

Great, now he could have some fun with the felines. "Here, kitty, kitty," Luca goaded.

"I'm not Jamie," Zak replied, his deep voice full of confidence. "I won't give you a chance to run."

Luca was having so much fun. "Keep a watch out for the felines and wolves while I watch for the bears and birds. If we have to run, remember to keep low to the ground and under cover," he told Abilene.

"Maybe we should shift?" she suggested.

He shook his head. He'd hold off on changing forms for now. Abilene would be able to get away easily enough. Her cheetah form would make it difficult for anyone to catch her speed. As a small coyote, Luca didn't have much chance of running away from the others. But he did have a few tricks up his sleeve. "Tell me when Zak's group reaches section four. I have another surprise for them."

He raised his own pair of binoculars to watch for Jamie. He should soon be reaching the curve next to the dry creek bed where Luca had placed a few smoke containers. He wouldn't risk actually hurting anyone, but the smoke would screw with their shifters senses. Make it harder to zero in on his location.

Movement caught his eye. Jamie stepped out from between two large trees while tilting his head back. He was still in human form, but Luca could tell that he was sniffing the area. Almost…to the traps.

Jamie waved at the team behind him, and Luca could hardly hold back his glee. Five steps and Jamie stepped on the release.

Three popping sounds alerted the bears before the canisters opened, filling the area with green smoke. Luca chuckled, and Jamie darted back under cover.

"Nice one," Jamie muttered. Luca couldn't have agreed more.

"They're almost to the fence," Abilene whispered to him.

Grabbing the right remote, Luca prepared for the shock and awe. He needed the felines to clear the area before all hell broke loosely behind them. "Tell me when," he ordered.

As she waited, Abilene was chewing on her bottom lip. He knew she enjoyed this game just as much as he did, although Abilene was always more cautious than him. "Just about..." she murmured.

He rubbed his hand over the green button.

"Now," Abilene said.

He hit the charge. The bang was loud and beautiful. Most people didn't know that the ATF was also in charge of regulating fireworks since they were considered explosives. Because of his job, he'd been able to secure some large firework displays to use. The sky filled with colourful streaks as the eruption occurred.

"That was just cool," Jamie praised over the headset. Of course he wasn't the one closet to that detonation so Luca suspected that had a lot to do with his enjoyment.

The roar that carried across the training field was long, loud and pissed off. Zak's tiger roar echoed and Luca had to suppress his instinct to cower down to the more dominant shifter. Luca's job was to make this exercise as difficult as possible. He needed to keep the shifters on their toes.

"Damn it, Luca," Abilene groused. "Now you've done it."

It wasn't easy making the very solid and calm Zak Lewis lose control. Luca prided himself on his accomplishment.

"We got you now," Jamie told him.

"I don't think so," Luca quipped back. But Jamie's confidence did worry him a little. He glanced over at Abilene, and she shrugged.

"Abilene, darling," Jamie drawled. "Why don't you get out of there while we teach your partner a lesson?"

"How about you get back to your mission? I don't have all night to wait for you. I do have other plans, you know," she replied.

Luca grinned—that was his girl. She always had his back.

"Fine, don't say I didn't warn you," Jamie said.

"Watch closely," Luca murmured. "They're up to something."

"Got it. I can't see Zak or the wolves," she told him.

Luca had lost sight of his targets, too. He squinted, hoping to pick up some sort of movement. He couldn't let himself forget that these were trained agents he was up against.

They had either retreated or were trying to find another path to where he and Abilene were hidden. He lifted his face as he breathed deeply. He couldn't pick up anything other than the dirty metallic scent from his explosives. While that aided him in his mission, the downside was that he couldn't smell if anyone was approaching.

Ten minutes went by and Luca had to force himself not to fidget. It was taking too long. The teams hadn't appeared back into view and there was complete radio silence.

The window of time left in which to find him and Abilene was quickly approaching. He hadn't actually thought that he would beat the Coalition in his first exercise. But now with—he glanced at his watch—a little over half an hour to go, he was certain of victory.

He leant closer to Abilene to whisper in her ear. She gasped, drawing his attention to the pack of wolves heading straight for them. Luca scrambled for his extra detonator. Several loud screeches made him look up as the birds of prey unit scooped down out of the air.

"Run," he ordered Abilene as he pushed her towards the right. If she went that way she'd be able to double back and get away. Hopefully into the middle of the training field where there was debris to hide in.

She took off. Luca was sure that she'd quickly be able to find a place to quickly shift. Well, at least one of them would get away. That was a win in his book.

The air around him shook as a long low growl came from behind him. Luca turned his head to see Zak stalking towards him. "Hey, buddy." Luca raised his hands in surrender and he climbed to his knees. "You're not really upset about the fireworks, are you?"

Zak lunged forward. Luca had just enough space to leap back onto a large boulder. There was movement to his right, and he ducked in time to avoid Jamie's large paw coming at his head.

He stumbled, but was able to keep his footing. "Oh, come on, guys!" he cried. "It was just a joke."

Zak growled in response. Since he was truly blocked off from escape, Luca knew he was beat. He dropped down to sit where he had been standing. "Fine, you win."

Jamie ambled over to him in his full black bear form. Luca held himself, still trusting that Jamie wouldn't really hurt him. Jamie's knock to his shoulder had him tilting over a little. Then Jamie sat on the ground right next to him, giving Luca his weight.

Thrilled to be able to bond with his brother in arms, he patted Jamie's massive back. "You have to admit it was a little funny," Luca teased. "You should have seen your face when the smoke bombs went off."

Jamie huffed, causing Luca to laugh. He glanced up at Zak who was starting to back away while shaking his head. This was only the second time Luca had seen Zak in his shifted form. He didn't know the entire story, but Abilene had shared with Luca a little about

Zak's past. Zak had been abused by his dad and uncle who had made him fight for his life every weekend.

It wasn't until Zak had started to let Abilene in and trust her that he'd been able to shift around anyone else. But Zak was still wary about transforming around others so Luca understood. He admired the strong, kind man that Zak had become. Luca couldn't have asked for a better mate for his partner.

Running his palm over Jamie's muzzle, Luca was proud to call these agents his friends. They were protective of one another and always supportive. As tough as Jamie appeared he was really a great guy. Big and tattooed, Jamie presented a front to the rest of the world—big bad biker, and you'd better watch out. On the inside Jamie was more of a teddy bear than a black bear. He was in love with a sweet, soft-spoken human whom Jamie worshipped. He was addicted to Coca-Cola and, given too much caffeine, bounced off the walls.

A soft rumble of contentment started at Jamie's chest as he relaxed against Luca.

"Come on, big guy, let's get you shifted and call it a night," Luca suggested.

Jamie struggled up before staggering off into the trees. Luca followed behind at a slower pace to give Jamie privacy to turn back into a human.

The training had gone well, even though he'd been found. He felt as though he'd been able to show the Coalition what he could offer and how they needed to improve. As their enemies grew in numbers, both shifters and humans, the Coalition had to step up their game. That was one of the main reasons that Luca had wanted the transfer to the Coalition. Not only did he feel more comfortable around them, but Luca also really believed that he could make a difference.

Only time would tell, though. A month into the Coalition and the ATF joint task force and they still had a lot of work to do. The unit was working on closing the last case that involved the Coalition and the ATF. The SIP—Shifters in Power—had more members out there in hiding. In the past few weeks the Coalition had managed to round up quite a group, but still the threat existed.

Luca was ready to put that mission behind him. He was just worried that when he was pulled from it he would also have to leave the Coalition. Or join them on a permanent basis. But that was a decision for another day.

Jumping over a boulder, he spotted the rest of the teams. His gaze automatically sought out Abilene to make sure she was safe. Zak had his arm wrapped around her shoulder while he nuzzled her neck. He'd lost count of the number of times he'd found the couple of after they'd shifted back to human form in a deep embrace before they were able to make it to privacy.

Luca understood the primal reaction that occurred after shifting and he was glad that he hadn't transformed that evening. It had been only him and his right hand for far too long. He actually hadn't got laid since before he'd taken his undercover job. *Wow!* When he thought about it that way, the months really added up.

"You up for a drink?" Calvin Hart called out to him as he approached the group. "These old bastards have to get home and into bed." He waved over at Zak, Abilene, Jamie and Cody.

"We won't be going there alone," Jamie replied with a huge grin. "Unlike you sad fuckers."

Calvin groaned good-naturedly. Luca slung his arm over his buddie's shoulder. When Calvin had been tending the bar he and Zak had visited while undercover Luca never would have guessed that the young shifter was an agent. He just didn't fit the typical federal agent stereotype. Calvin was more surfer dude than bad cop. Luca had liked him immediately, though. As Calvin was another of the single agents, Luca also spent a lot of time with him. "I'm in," Luca told him. "I could use a cold one. You can tell me how Zak jumped like a little girl when the fireworks went off."

Zak flipped Luca his middle finger but didn't remove his lips from Abilene's neck.

"Let's get him out of here," Jamie said to Cody while pointing at Zak.

Cody chuckled before grabbing Zak's shoulder. Luca turned back to Calvin. "I've got a change of clothes in my truck. I'll meet you at the pub."

"Sounds good."

Looking forward to a relaxing brew, Luca took off in a jog towards his Chevy Silverado. He'd left it unlocked with the keys under the seat since he hadn't wanted to carry any more supplies than he needed. Slinging his pack onto the back seat, he took a deep breath. The soft breeze brought forward the salt from the lake close by.

He loved Lake Worth, Arizona. It was a large city with a small town feel. A lot of shifters had gravitated to the area after they'd become public to have the sense of safety in numbers. His own home was only an hour away but being in Lake Worth really made him feel at home.

Like when he'd been younger.

Luca was extremely lucky to have a wonderful large family. Both his parents were warm and loving, and his siblings, while they drove him crazy, also showed their own support. It wasn't always easy being part of such a close band of coyotes but Luca wouldn't trade any of them for any amount of money in the world.

Well maybe Sal, his oldest brother. Salvatore Perez was loud, brash, and too damn arrogant. Sal had decided long ago that when their father wasn't close by he would be in charge. Over Luca's loud and passionate objections, their dad had agreed.

Sal called every week to check up on him. When Luca had been shot on his last assignment, Sal had dragged his partner with him to make sure that Luca was okay. While it annoyed him the way that Sal ordered him around, he also never doubted that he was loved.

Shaking his thoughts away, he got back to the business of changing clothes. He was dirty and sweaty. He yanked his black T-shirt over his head then exchanged it for a white one. He popped the button of his jeans before unzipping them. Quickly he replaced those with his favourite faded pair. They were loosely and comfortable, the denim thin from multiple washes.

Luckily, he had also packed wet wipes and gave himself a quick brush with them so he felt a little more refreshed. He wasn't looking for a date tonight, but if he happened to see a woman who caught his attention, he didn't want to stink.

He stuffed his dirty clothing back into the duffel before slamming the door closed. Climbing into the front seat, he reached down to pull out his key ring. He was so ready for a cold one. He climbed behind the wheel and started the vehicle. The teams always went to the same bar when they went out. It welcomed both humans and shifters. The owner and bartenders were fully human but they had got to know the Coalition well.

It was a short five minutes until Luca was pulling up in front of the lit-up sign. Calvin stood out front by the door smoking a cigarette. Luca shook his head. Calvin had started that habit while undercover during the last assignment they'd shared. Zak might have been the agent in danger along with Luca, but Calvin had also been involved.

Calvin had posed as a bartender where the SIP went to do their drinking. It had been a good way for Zak and Calvin to pass information back to base. And the two of them were good. Luca had almost always been at Zak's side and he'd never picked up on the fact that Zak and Calvin knew each other and that both worked for the Coalition.

He climbed out of his truck to stroll towards his friend.

"Hey, man," Calvin greeted. "Thanks for meeting me. I've got too much adrenaline to hit the sack so soon. Man, I hate night exercises. It screws with my whole system."

"I know what you mean. I still haven't got back on track since I've come off my undercover assignment so it's not too bad for me. Abilene was bitching the other day about it, but Zak assured her that he'd make sure she sleeps like a baby."

They both laughed at that. Zak had fallen so hard and fast for Abilene that Luca knew it was just a matter of time before they were committed to each other. Maybe even mated.

Even though Zak and Abilene were two different species of cat—Zak being a tiger and Abilene a cheetah shifter — they made a dynamic couple of. They were a match in every possible way. Luca hoped he'd be able to find someone like that for himself. He'd never really considered settling down until he'd seen how happy those around him were.

He had some issues, he could admit. Could even be a little childish at times, like during the exercise earlier that evening, but he hoped that someone could see past that and love him for all his faults.

"I'll buy the first round," Luca told Calvin as he slapped him on the back.

"Sounds good," Calvin said. He stubbed out the end of his cig before tossing it into the trash. Luca held open the door and let Calvin walk in first.

Luca followed behind and scanned the room like he'd been trained. The bar wasn't too busy. Half a dozen patrons sat at the bar drinking from bottles and glasses. Four tables held bigger groups as they laughed and talked. He motioned with his head to one of the tall tables in the back. It would give them a good view of both the front door and the entrance from the hall.

He was never off duty. If there was trouble, he and Calvin would be ready for it. They passed a group of three women who all turned their heads to eye the new meat that had arrived. He checked them out the same as they were doing to him and Calvin.

The full-chested blonde had a ring on her left finger so he scanned her quickly before moving on to the redhead to her right. She was small in stature, probably no taller than five-five, with an ample bosom and a very pretty face. The third woman had dirty blonde short hair and pretty blue eyes but his gaze went back to the redhead as he walked up behind her.

She smiled up at him before slowly dropping her gaze in flirtation. Oh yeah, a drink had been a wonderful idea.

"Hello, ladies," Calvin greeted as they continued to stroll on.

He received a giggle in response. So they were probably well on the way to being drunk. Luca hoped that they weren't too blasted. He had no problem with picking up a woman at a bar, but he did want her to remember the night they spent together.

Calvin yanked one of the tall chairs out and sat. Luca did the same. Rosalinda, the pretty Spanish waitress that they'd come to know, was at their side right away.

"What's it going to be, boys?" she asked.

"Couple of drafts and two shots of tequila," Calvin requested. "Why don't you send that table over there a refill also?"

Rosalinda glanced behind her at the women. "You got it."

"You got the redhead?" Calvin leant forward and asked.

Yeah, Luca had a type and she fit it perfectly. He enjoyed being dominant in bed and wanted a partner that could appreciate his strength. He had to be careful, though, since he was much stronger than a human male. If he didn't watch it he could leave bruises. Some women didn't mind but Luca preferred not to go too hard when picking up a lady at a bar. Alcohol could do funny things to one's inhibitions and he never wanted someone to regret the time spent with him.

"Yep," he answered Calvin.

"I do love the blondes," Calvin said happily.

Luca laughed. Calvin was worse than he was. Luca didn't set out to pick up a girl every time he went out. Calvin, on the other hand, called the night a failure if he didn't get laid.

Rosalinda dropped off their drinks before continuing on to the ladies. Luca watched out of the corner of his eye as the three women accepted their offering before standing. Oh, he was so getting some tonight.

The redhead slipped to Luca's side and put her hand on his arm. "Thank you for the drink," she murmured seductively.

"You're very welcome," Luca told her. He wrapped his arm around her waist and pulled her close. There would be no question about what he wanted.

Calvin was already talking to the two blondes so Luca didn't feel rude for not striking up a conversation with them. "I'm Luca Perez."

"Beth Williams," she said while running her palm up the front of his shirt. He might be smaller than most of the shifters he was surrounded by on a daily basis, but Luca worked out hard and had nice muscles to show for it. He captured Beth's hand, pressing it against his heart. "And what are you up to this evening?"

"Just looking for a little fun," she told him boldly.

He smiled, picked up his shot and drank it quickly. "Me too."

Chapter Two

Jade Adams watched the video of the joint Coalition and ATF task force from the night before. As a behaviour analyst with the FBI she couldn't deny her interest in how the two very different agencies were working together. Even more so when her supervisor had informed her that the FBI would also like to add a few agents into the fold. Jade had quickly volunteered her and her partner for the job.

While she was pure human, she had been teamed up with a wolf shifter named Cole Babcock since she'd transferred into the Lake Worth office. Cole had ten years' experience on her and she'd learned a lot in the six months they'd been working side by side.

This opportunity was a chance for Cole to see how the Coalition worked. Jade was looking forward to learning more about the shifters and their behaviors.

From the beginning when she'd found out that some human beings could transform, she'd been drawn in. So much made sense now that she was able to connect someone's personality and shifting ability.

Turned out her brother was married to a fox shifter. Jimmy had known but had kept it from his family to protect his wife. Now Alice and Jade could openly mention Alice's other form. Jade had noticed a big difference in their relationship. Alice had confided in Jade that instead of feeling like an outsider who had always had secrets, she was comfortable around the entire Adams family.

Jade had grown closer to Jimmy as well. Since Jimmy's entire family had welcomed Alice with open arms when they'd discovered her secrets, Jimmy came around more often than he had been. Guilt had kept her brother from attending a lot of dinners and holidays. Jade felt as though she had her brother back. And she loved that.

Soon after Jade had learned of her brother's mate she had been asked to consult on a case with some agents from the Lake Worth office. Cole had strolled into the large conference room and announced that he was a wolf shifter. He was also heading up the team and if anyone had a problem with him they were free to leave.

She had been shocked when three agents had actually walked out of the door.

It wasn't until later when she'd been partnered with Cole for a month that he'd told her he'd been getting threats and taunts almost daily from agents who didn't like his shifter status. Even people who had once been his friends had turned their backs.

Pissed off on his behalf, she'd assured him that she had no issues at all. Cole had simply nodded before turning away.

Jade didn't take it personally, though. While it was taking longer than she wished, Cole was slowly opening up to her.

"You're watching that again?"

She turned her head to peer at her partner as he walked into her office. "We're meeting these guys today. I just want to make sure I'm ready."

Cole leant on the side of her desk to look over her shoulder at her monitor. "You're a good agent. You don't have anything to worry about."

Pleased with the compliment, she grinned. "Thanks but they're all shifters. I can't compete with that." It was her biggest fear. She wasn't able to run as fast, see as well, and she didn't have superior hearing.

"You'll probably be the smartest one in the room. And if they give you a hard time I'll take care of it."

Since Cole didn't give praise very often Jade knew he meant it. But that didn't help with her nerves. Plus she didn't want Cole to go into the meeting with aggression. If he felt that he had to protect her, Cole's alpha personality could make it difficult for the two of them to fit in with the Coalition. She wanted this partnership to work.

Glancing through the windowed wall into the rest of their department, she couldn't help but be disgusted with the people she worked with. Cole had proven to be experienced, dedicated and smart. He closed cases and put the bad guys behind bars. Yet there were only a handful of agents who sought out his advice. It was a shame.

He didn't even get support from their boss. Special Agent Jensen ignored them both unless he had a difficult case that he needed to be handled. Jade had noticed that over the last several months, every case that she and Cole were handed was a job that no one else wanted or that had the potential of real danger.

When she'd read about the joint task force through the intranet home page that the agents all shared, she'd submitted hers and Cole's names without asking their boss or her partner. It wasn't until they'd made the shortlist that she had come clean and informed Cole about what she'd done.

And hadn't that been a fun conversation. Not.

Cole hadn't blown up or anything, but he hadn't been happy either. Instead of being relieved at getting away from the jerks they shared an office with, Cole had calmly explained to her that he didn't want to go anywhere. He wanted the other agents to look at his face every day and know what he was.

She tried to understand but couldn't figure him out. She'd seen Cole turn the other cheek numerous times when someone would mumble under their breath about him being an animal or some other taunt. Cole never blew up or confronted them. Just kept walking like he didn't hear them. Except Jade knew he did. If *she* could pick up on the rude comments and gestures, Cole *had* to. But he really acted like he couldn't care less.

Jade wanted to throttle them all.

Instead, she'd worked on talking Cole into accepting the temporary joint task force assignment. She'd practically begged before he'd given in. Now they would finally get to work with others who would accept Cole. She couldn't wait to see how her partner reacted.

"We better get going if we don't want to be late," Cole interrupted her thoughts.

"I'm ready," she replied. She grabbed the messenger bag she'd packed earlier with notebooks, her laptop, a charger and office supplies.

"You remind me of a little kid getting to go see Santa," he teased. At least she thought he was just teasing. Sometimes she couldn't tell with him.

Instead of commenting, she grabbed her suit jacket off the back of her chair and slipped it on, covering her weapon and badge in the process. She'd gone with power grey for her wardrobe that morning. The dark pants and matching jacket were complemented with a light blue silk shirt. Her boots were both comfortable and fashionable and were the same colour as her suit.

She pulled her shoulder-length brown hair up into a clip with a few strands flowing loosely. She wanted to appear professional but easy to work with. She absolutely didn't want to come across as eager as she was. Following behind Cole, she locked her office before walking with him to the elevator.

Jade didn't miss the looks of disgust on a few faces as they passed. Cole walked with his shoulders back, head up and expression clear. She was going to have to learn how he did that. Practice in a mirror or something.

She sighed in relief when the elevator opened immediately for them. She didn't enjoy feeling her co-worker's eyes boring into the back of her head.

"Ignore them," Cole whispered as they both stepped inside.

Jade grinned. "I'm trying. I just want to punch them in the throat."

Cole snorted out a laugh that was so unexpected that Jade turned to stare at him.

"What?" he groused, when he noticed.

"Nothing," she replied but didn't stop smiling. Yeah, Cole was coming around. She was even almost certain that he liked her.

"Whatever," he muttered, but Jade was sure he was keeping himself from smiling too. She didn't want to push her luck, though, so she remained silent.

"I'll drive," he said when the doors opened to the parking garage.

Once again Jade didn't reply. Like there was any doubt that he would take the wheel. He never let her drive.

He hit the key fob to his department SUV, disarming the alarm and unlocking the doors. She stashed her bag in the back seat. Cole's backpack was already inside. Maybe he was more excited than he was letting on. Normally he let her handle the paperwork, but if he was bringing his computer he might just surprise her.

She climbed into the passenger seat. "Have you ever met any of the agents?" she asked him. Out of all of their talks about the Coalition she'd never asked that. He might be more comfortable if he knew the teams already.

"No," he replied. "From what I gather the Coalition doesn't get along any better with the FBI than anyone else."

The way the Feds were treating her partner made Jade feel like the Coalition might have a reason for not getting along with them. "We'll change their minds," she said.

Cole shook his head. He pulled out of his parking spot and drove to the exit before he spoke. "Just because this agency is made up of shifters doesn't mean they're not assholes," he warned. "You need to be careful what you tell them until we know we can trust them."

Jade didn't like it but she knew her partner was right. "I will. I just want to see how all the different shifter species work together."

"I'm curious about that myself," he admitted.

"Really?"

He hummed as he merged with traffic.

Jade waited. Or at least she tried. "Why?" she asked when Cole didn't continue.

"I watched the video from last night too. Not only do the teams work together but alpha personalities seem to be able to operate together without any problems. I've never been around many shifters — my pack and family along with a few other agents — but these are very predatory creatures who function well in their missions."

"You're the one that tells me you're simply a human with special abilities," she reminded him. "Wouldn't that reasoning apply to them also?"

"Yes and no. I am human. But I also have a part of me that needs to be in control. The dominant gene that won't allow me to bow down to anyone who isn't as strong."

"Maybe it's different for wolf shifters?" she offered.

"I don't think so. One of the teams was made up of my kind. Then you had birds of prey, felines and bears. All aggressive traits. One of the reasons I agreed to this crazy joint unit was to get an inside perspective on how they work. Even if this doesn't work out in the long run, which I don't think it will, hopefully I can pick up something that will help me later on down the road."

She didn't comment on his insistence that the task force wouldn't work. He'd been saying that from the beginning. Getting a look at the Coalition and the ATF in training had her believing the opposite. But he did have a point about the other species and their animal parts. She'd been studying shifter behaviors since she'd first been given access. Of course, most of her theories were based on shifters who were criminals, but she still felt strongly that the human shifter did carry over several traits that affected how they handled certain situations.

"Wait—You said you've been around other agents who shift. Which ones?" she asked. As far as she knew Cole was the only shifter who worked in the office. Of course the FBI was a huge organisation and was everywhere in the United States, but it had a smaller branch in Lake Worth than in other major cities.

"Sorry but I can't tell you that. If they want to come out I'll support them—I've already let them know—but as long as they want to remain hidden, I will keep their secret," he said.

Jade leant back in her seat and crossed her arms. She didn't like that answer but she knew the tone that Cole was using. He wouldn't tell her. "You know," she accused.

He tapped the side of his nose.

"Oh well." That made sense. Cole could tell whether they were fully human or not without anyone having to say a word. He could scent them. It helped when they were in the field but at that moment it gave him information she didn't have. That annoyed her.

"You're about to get your fill of shifters." Cole glanced over at her. "Stop pouting."

"I'm not pouting," she argued. Oh, she was, but she wouldn't give him the satisfaction of agreeing.

"Sure," he consented.

She punched his arm. He didn't even act as though her hit affected him. She'd have to work out more. It was only fair, after all, that she was as strong as possible to protect him as much as he did her since they were partners. Not that she would actually say that. Cole would probably just laugh at her if she did. "You're not worried that they'll resent us since we're Feds, are you?" Since the shifters had announced themselves publicly the FBI had actually come out to denounce them. Jade hated that.

"It's possible. You're a human FBI agent. I'll be making sure no one gives you a hard time. Don't worry," he said.

She huffed. "I can take care of myself too, you know."

"You're a human going into an organisation that is full of predators who don't have a lot of respect for where we come from. Stay by my side and follow my lead," Cole ordered.

"Yes, sir," she replied cheekily. He knew her well enough—if someone challenged her she wouldn't back down.

"Remember all that you've learned," he told her. "Most will be okay but there will be very dominant shifters who will have no problem trying to put you in your place."

"That where you come in?" she guessed.

"Yes," he replied seriously. "I am more up to their speed. Some won't even question you because you're my partner. That doesn't mean we'll be safe, though. Just follow my lead and we'll be fine."

"You don't think this will work, do you?" she questioned.

"No, it's not that," Cole said with a shake of his head. "I just have a lot on my mind. I actually do hope to learn more about how the Coalition works. I think it will be beneficial if our bosses ever get their heads out of their asses."

She so hated that Cole had to fight to be at the office every day to do his job. "Sometimes I don't know why you do it," she told him.

"If I don't, who will?" he asked. "Besides, it's better to be on the inside than out and not being able to do anything."

She could agree with that statement. "So," she said to change the subject, "did you see how that ATF agent scared the crap out of the bear shifter team?"

"You liked that, did you?" he asked while smiling.

"Of course. Admit it, so did you."

"I would probably have beaten his ass if he'd done it to me," Cole said. "But yeah, it was fun to see."

"If this task force works maybe I can find out some more about the behaviors. Are all coyote shifters crazy like Luca Perez appears, or is it just him?"

"I've actually met a few and I have to say that I think this Luca guy is unique," Cole informed her.

"Huh."

"You sound disappointed," he pointed out.

"No, not really. I was just hoping to learn more."

"Have you decided what you are going to do with all your research?" he questioned. "Maybe write a book?"

"Oh no, I'm no writer. I want to help update the training manual, though. I have a friend who is at the agency and he asked to see a couple of of my papers. He thought it would be a good idea so he knew what the shifters could do and not waste time. I mean they are going to be faster, stronger and better at a lot of the physical stuff. He hoped I might be able to come up with a procedure to really utilise their skills. He was also worried that as a human he might put them at risk and wanted to avoid that."

"That actually sounds like a wonderful idea," Cole complimented. "I was bored so much of the time. The physical tests for shifters is too easy and wastes available time. But I really could have used more time in other areas like the classroom work. Shifters do think differently than humans and since we couldn't reveal our shifter sides yet I really had to work hard on passing the written portion test."

"Well, maybe I'll come up with something," she said, pleased that her work might just help.

"I'll bet you can." Cole smiled at her. "We're almost there."

* * * *

"But why do we have to work with the damn feebies?" Jamie whined.

Luca hid his smile behind his hand. No one liked working with the FBI—or feebies, if he wanted to insult them. The FBI had been the one government branch that hadn't welcomed shifters into their fold with open arms. Luca had inside knowledge on how the FBI treated their shifter agents since his brother worked in a branch in California.

"If we want to change how people view us but can't get our own federal agencies on board, how do you think that will work?" Commander Green questioned Jamie.

Jamie sighed. "Fine."

"We'll have four agents joining us. Two local and two from out east. I expect everyone to work with them. This joint force will be a success," Commander Green said. "If I get one negative comment from anyone already in the unit that person will be sorry."

Luca had never been witness to one of Commander Green's dressing downs, but he had heard about them. The man was a powerful ally, but he didn't want to get on his bad side.

"They'll behave," Cody assured the boss.

Jamie stuck his tongue out at Cody. Beside him, Abilene tried to stifle a giggle but failed. Zak casually leant forward and smacked Jamie in the back of the head. Luca bit his tongue as Jamie grunted.

"Make sure," Green told Cody. "The locals will be here today. The other two won't arrive until sometime tonight so I have them reporting at 0700 hours sharp tomorrow."

"So what exactly do you want us to show them?" Zak questioned.

"That's up to you. The locals have one shifter and one human. The others are both human. They need to see how we plan and carry out operations, but I wouldn't mind them getting some training and fieldwork too. This programme is important to ensure that we all *can* and *will* work together." Commander Green nodded to Cody. "Talk it over and keep me informed. I'll send the agents to you when they arrive."

"If you bring in the CIA next, I'm quitting," Jamie called out to him.

"Don't tempt me," Green shot back.

Luca waited until Commander Green had left before throwing his pen at Jamie.

"What?" Jamie cried with innocence. He held his hands up. "I was just making a point!"

Abilene snorted, Zak grunted and Luca shook his head. One of the reasons Luca enjoyed working with Jamie so much was because of his playful attitude. Oh, Jamie could be fierce, and when he was working in the field he was good. He was an awesome agent. Afterward, when it was just them hanging out, Jamie made Luca relax and laugh.

He knew he was too serious most of the time. Abilene had been telling him that for years. Now that he was spending time with Jamie and the other agents he could see what she meant. Just because they joked around didn't mean that they didn't take their assignments seriously. They just needed the break sometimes.

"Getting back on point," Cody stated loudly, standing, "what should we do with the agents?"

"Well—" Jamie started.

"Enough!" Zak barked, pointing at him. Jamie sat back with his lower lip sticking out.

"You're still working with the district attorney this week on the SIP case, right?" Zak asked Cody.

"Yeah, my team's booked with wrapping this up today. I can attend some late afternoons or evening ops anytime, though, no matter what. I'm really hoping to be finished by the end of the day," Cody confirmed.

Luca winced in sympathy. It was a good thing that he and Zak hadn't had to take the paperwork side of the mission. But since the case relied on his and Zak's testimony, they couldn't work on the conviction process. They were witnesses. Luca was grateful. Cop work, even with the government, had too damn much paperwork. Cody spent his days signing, submitting and preparing forms. It sucked to be him.

"That might work out better. I want to see how the two locals work together. A human and a shifter partnered up. It should give them an advantage against other teams with only human members," Zak said.

"It's different for our team. Both Luca and I are shifters and I didn't partner with a human before. I like working with Luca since we are so in sync. We have a great success rate with our cases. I wonder how the two Feds do."

Now that was a good question. Luca was curious also. This might not be too bad a test.

"I'd like to set up an exercise for a couple of nights from now. Test both teams along with ourselves," Zak said. "We could use more training and still need to work out any kinks on how we operate."

"Let me do it," Jamie jumped up.

Luca glanced at Abilene — the expression on her face wasn't any less concerned than how he felt.

Zak was shaking his head.

"Oh, come on," Jamie argued. "You know my training drill will test not only them but us too. What, you want to leave the crazy explosives guy in charge?" he asked, pointing back at Luca.

Luca raised his hands. "I said I was sorry."

"You just wait," Jamie warned. "You won't know when, or where, but I will get you back."

Abilene placed her hand on his shoulder. She always did have Luca's back. "Is that a threat?" she asked super sweetly.

"No, baby, that's a promise," Jamie taunted.

Zak growled, causing Jamie to spin towards him. "I was just kidding," Jamie told him.

Luca could tell that Zak was only a few seconds away from smacking Jamie again. Which would lead to the two of them either boxing in the gym or rolling around right there.

He was relieved when Abilene patted his shoulder and headed towards her boyfriend. She wrapped her arm around his waist. Zak didn't hesitate in embracing her back.

"It's okay. I know his weak spot. I've got Brandy on speed dial."

Jamie groaned as everyone else laughed at his expense. Luca felt more at home with this group than he'd ever felt at his own agency. The ATF wasn't as bad as the FBI but there were still some assholes around who tried to give him and Abilene a hard time.

The ATF also paired shifters together. A shifter and a human was an interesting dynamic and he was curious to see how they worked. "I think I have an idea about how to test them," he said.

Everyone in the room groaned.

"I promise to leave my bag of tricks at home," he stated. He didn't see why Zak and Jamie were still upset. He hadn't actually blown them up, after all.

"What are you thinking?" Zak questioned.

"How about we split up into two groups? Have two feebies on one side and the other two against them. We'll also divide our ranks. That way we can see how they think," Luca suggested.

"That sounds good." Abilene grinned at him. "How about a rescue mission? Luca can be the bait."

"Why me?" he bitched.

"Because if anyone can get along with the Feds it will be you," Abilene told him.

"Fine," Luca agreed. "But we need to make it interesting."

"Let's figure this out," Zak ordered.

Luca pulled out his notepad and started to make notes. He loved the planning stages of an exercise. He wanted to add more than just having to be rescued, though. If the team that kidnapped him had more to their mission, it could make things interesting.

Jamie and Calvin were throwing out ideas about how to track him if for some reason Luca was rescued.

"I love being the bad guy." Jamie clapped his hands.

Oh God, Jamie was going to be a handful the entire time that the Feds were here. More so than he normally was.

Chapter Three

Jade was really trying to play it cool but she was in awe as she toured the building that housed the Shifter Coalition Agency. The newly remodeled structure was state of the art and such an improvement from where she was normally stationed. The FBI didn't provide anything like the Coalition.

Not only were there large office spaces that the teams shared, but also several conference and integration rooms. That was in addition to a new gym, a cafeteria and awesome locker rooms. She was very impressed. She glanced over at Cole to try to gauge his reaction. Her partner had nodded a few times but hadn't said anything. She was dying to know what he really thought.

"The other teams involved in this joint task force are waiting for you. Cody Johnson and his team—the birds of prey division—aren't available as they're still trying to wrap up the final details of our last case, but the others are in the conference room," Commander Green said.

So far Jade was getting a good feeling from Commander Green. He had shaken both their hands and invited to show them around. He had spoken a little about what he hoped to accomplish but hadn't grilled them about why they'd volunteered to be a part of this new force.

Jade was aware of what most other agencies, especially shifter organisations, thought about the FBI. She hoped to change their opinions, though.

"Did you get a chance to watch the videos I sent you of the training exercises we've run?" Green asked.

"Yes, sir," she replied for both of them. "The teams seem to be working well together already." She'd viewed the data Green had provided numerous times. She was just a little obsessed.

"I believe they are," he agreed. "It just shows what putting the right people in place can accomplish."

"Yes, sir," she agreed.

"If you need anything please don't hesitate to get in touch with me," Green offered. "Here we are." He led them to a closed door and knocked.

He didn't wait for the door to open but pushed it himself. Jade peeked through his arm to see a collection of men and a few women standing around. She recognised them from the video she'd watched the previous evening.

Cole was at her back as she stepped farther into the room. "Hi." She waved. It was only after the big guy—Jamie, if she remembered correctly—snorted that she realised she probably looked like an idiot. Rolling her shoulders, she held her head up high and met Jamie's gaze.

Jade would not be intimated by him. She knew he was a brown bear shifter but she had a bad ass wolf at her back. He stared her down for a couple of of seconds before laughing and grinning. She returned his smile. Cole was standing stiffly behind her. She reached and grabbed hold of his arm. She wanted the other agents to see that they were a team and to keep Cole calm. If he thought anyone in the room was a threat to her he would be aggressive. "I'm Jade and this is my partner Cole."

The big bear shifter was the first one to approach. He held out his hand to Jade first. She shook and was pleased when he didn't try to crush her hand. Some men, even humans, liked to attempt to put her in her place. Not that it ever worked. She was an outgoing and strong female. And proud of it.

Cole followed her lead, exchanging introductions as the others came forward.

If she hadn't studied the videos there wouldn't have been any way that she would have remembered all their names. Mentally she matched up their names, faces and shifter animal.

The last agent she met was the male ATF coyote shifter. He was only a few inches taller than her so when they shook she met his gaze. He was a good-looking guy. He had dark hair and eyes along with a bronze completion.

"Hi," she greeted.

"Luca Perez," he replied. "I'm part of the ATF joint task force. It's nice to meet you."

"You too," she said. Reluctantly she let go of his hand. She didn't know why but there was something about him that she was drawn to more than anyone else in the room. She didn't know much about natural coyote traits but she was pretty sure that they were a close relative of wolves. It made her wonder if he was as dominant as her partner.

"Let's sit for a few minutes and discuss how we'd like to move forward," Zak Lewis suggested.

Jade followed Luca back to the long conference table and sat beside him. She was interested in getting to know him better. Cole remained by her side and sat to her right. She glanced over at her partner and noticed him watching her.

She lifted an eyebrow but instead of answering her unspoken question he just shrugged. She'd have to get with him later and see what that look on his face was about.

"We're already planning some training exercises to include you both in but we'll wait until the other FBI agents arrive," Zak told them.

"What other agents?" she asked. As far as she knew, only Cole and she had been given this task.

"There are two more feebies joining us. They won't be here until tomorrow, though. They're flying in from out east," Jamie supplied.

Jade suspected that Jamie was purposely baiting her and Cole to see if they responded to the offensive term used for the FBI. She was certain there would be no reaction from Cole so she peered over at Jamie and smiled. "I wasn't aware that four of us had been chosen." In the memo she'd received from headquarters they'd asked for two agents to volunteer. Jade didn't mind sharing the task force — well that wasn't entirely true she wanted the experience, but if more agents would help get others at the FBI to accept shifters she wouldn't complain. She glanced over at Cole but he only shrugged. Since Cole didn't seem worried she'd try not to be either. "I thought it was just Cole and me."

Jamie shrugged in response. "It's not like our bosses tell us any more than I imagine you're informed."

"Hmm, okay. If we're not going into any training today, maybe you can start off with some cases you've worked. I'd like to get an idea of how your organisation operates," she said.

"Sure," Jamie agreed.

She leant forward as he started to tell her about some cases the Coalition had worked in the last year. The unit under Cody Johnson concentrated on homicides either of shifters or committed by shifters.

"How does the local police department feel about you taking over their cases?" she asked.

"The same as when anyone else sticks their noses in," Jamie replied. "We've become friends with a couple of of the detectives. Cody even had them come on during his investigation to smooth over any hurt feelings."

"Okay good. Please continue," she requested. This was what she was looking for. She was busy taking notes as Jamie spoke. Hopefully later they would give her access to their files and she could dig deeper.

As she worked she was very aware of Luca by her side. He went back and forth between watching her and giving his attention to Jamie. A couple of of times he moved his leg and it brushed up against her. The heat she felt from his body was distracting but she tried her best to push that aside. He was even more attractive than she'd assumed by watching him in action.

Considering her experience with shifters, she was shocked by how comfortable she was in the room with everyone. She relaxed as she continued to listen and learn all she could about the Coalition. Even Cole seemed to be more at ease than she'd seen him in a good while. She was so pleased with how the first hour had passed. Oh, she was sure they'd still be testing her and Cole, but Jade knew she was up for the challenge. This was going to rock.

* * * *

"Keep your head down and follow my lead," Cole whispered to her.

Jade glanced over at him and caught his gaze before nodding. The exercise seemed pretty straightforward but after viewing what the task force was capable of during training she expected a few traps.

The wolf shifter unit—Mitch, Brady and Adam—would provide backup for them. Jade had been surprised when the wolves had been assigned to them but Cole had only nodded before taking the lead. According to Jamie the wolves were mainly used to assist all the other teams. They knew how the birds, felines and bears worked, so that intel would be a great help for them.

The two other FBI agents were sent to guard Luca. It had been Zak's suggestion that the human feds stay with the majority of the Coalition for this mission. Since they hadn't done the same homework as she and Cole had, the two special agents, Patrick Connelly and Sam Westby, lacked advantage of knowing what they were up against.

"Luca is explosives happy," Mitch said from behind them.

Jade laughed. "I noticed that. So the house will probably be rigged?"

"Oh yeah," Mitch agreed.

Jade liked the younger shifter. He was tall and broad-shouldered with an easy smile. He reminded her of her little brother Jules. She slowed down so that Mitch could join them. "What else?"

"Cody's team will be lookout. They'll be in their shifted form and will circle around the target," Mitch provided.

They reached the van that they were to use. Cole yanked open the back door and motioned everyone forward. The small parking garage light washed over them as they gathered closer to Cole. There were five of them. Cole and Jade, and three shifters—Mitch, Brady and Adam. The other teams were guarding the location and the target, Luca.

"They expect a sneak attack," Cole stated. "Luca isn't allowed to fight back if we catch him. He has to come willingly. So we just have to catch the security teams off guard."

"This is impossible," Adam stated. "They work together too well. We'll never get close to Luca."

Jade shook her head. "No, because they still have to follow the rules. Only one team is allowed to remain with Luca in the house. The others have to play along as if they have other work to continue. I think they'll break the teams up, though. For the first shift they'll have a bird, bear and feline and keep rotating."

"I agree," Cole said. He glanced at his watch. "We have six minutes until the mission starts. We need to be ready to move quickly. We have the address they'll be at so that's the easiest part. He grabbed a long tube from the back of the vehicle. "Jade, you and Mitch look at the prints from the house. They are going to expect us to hit between one and three so that's what we're not going to do."

"Why one and three?" Brady asked. Brady was the newest member of the Coalition, Jade had learned, only joining the wolves a month ago. He'd just got his criminal justice degree but didn't have a lot of field experience. He was, however, very determined to prove himself. Jade had noticed that he stayed quiet when all the task force were together and hung back. He was an observer. She respected that trait and knew that it would come in handy.

"Because that's normally when we would strike. The guards will be getting tired. That's the shift they'll give to Cody, Zak and Jamie. Those three will be tough to beat. They have the most training and have worked together for a long time. We want to avoid them if at all possible," Cole said.

"You want to hit them right away," Jade guessed.

"Yes," Cole replied. "The problem with that is after we get Luca we'll have to hide him. This exercise is to run until 0500 hours. If we get Luca the others have a chance to retrieve him back. We don't want that so we need a safe house."

Jade bit her lip as she considered their options. Cole had a point that hitting the target house early would give them an advantage but there was no way that they could hide Luca for seven hours without a plan. "We could bring him back here," she suggested as she waved to the Coalition office behind her.

"They'll expect that. And they know the building better than we do," Cole said.

"The FBI safe house?" Mitch suggested.

Cole nodded. "I thought about that but I think that would be their second choice. Sam and Patrick could easily find out where it was located. They have enough manpower to break up and hit both places."

"They'll also be able to access the FBI since they have two agents with them," Jade stated.

"So we need a house?" Adam asked.

Jade glanced over at him. He was grinning with a little bit of an evil glint to his eye. "What?" she questioned, afraid of his answer.

"I have an idea," he said before laughing. "But they're gonna be pissed off."

Cole grinned. "I like it already," Cole told him. "Where?"

"Some place they'd never think to look but we know will be empty," Adam said. "Zak's house."

"Are you crazy!" Mitch exclaimed.

"I don't think that's a good idea," Brady agreed. "He'll kill us for sure."

"Think about it. Zak and Abilene are both on the mission. We've been to his house several times for cookouts and know the layout. The neighbours won't think anything weird about government vehicles being around. It's perfect."

It really did seem like the best solution. She peered over at her partner, not surprised to see Cole's gaze lit with excitement. Her partner hadn't been butting heads with the tiger shifter but there was tension between the two with both being so dominant. Cole had assured her that it wouldn't be a problem, but Jade could see that Cole loved the idea of hiding out at the man's home.

Cole started to laugh. "Perfect."

"Oh, this is *so* not a good idea," Jade commented. Brady was nodding while Mitch and Adam continued to grin.

"We'll go there first. Get the lay of the land and make sure it is empty. He could have friends over or something. But if the place is empty, I say we use it," Cole said. He tossed the keys to Adam. "You drive."

She climbed inside the back of the van in front of the rest of her team. Cole was the last inside. As soon as he had slammed the doors the vehicle took off.

She settled on the seat and made room for him. "You know this could blow up in our face," she whispered.

He turned his head. "It'll be fine. You've seen how close these guys are and they have a pretty good sense of humour. I think they'll appreciate our genius."

Jade drew back to really look Cole over. "You like them." She couldn't have been more shocked. Her partner hadn't wanted to be part of this trial and had only agreed for her.

Cole leant closer again. "Not as much as you," he said.

"What?" Damn, that had come out as a squeak.

"Did you think I missed how you were eyeing Luca? Or that I don't know when you find someone attractive?" Cole teased. He bumped her shoulder. "I know my partner."

She ducked her head, sure that she was blushing. She hadn't expected to be called on her fascination with Luca so soon. "I don't know —"

Cole threw his arm over her shoulder. "It's okay. I actually like him best myself. He's smart, strong and a little crazy. A great match for you."

She elbowed him. Cole'd never acted like this before. The teasing was completely new. In the last two days he'd opened up and played around, laughing and joking. She liked this new side of her partner. "Whatever," she mumbled.

He removed his arm but the heat around her neck remained. She felt good knowing that Cole really did like her. She'd tried so hard to be an equal and always have his back. It hadn't been easy when they'd been at the office since Cole was always suspicious of the agents around them. Here at the Coalition it seemed as though he didn't have to hide and could let his true self out. More and more, she hoped that this joint task force would work and that they'd be picked to join it permanently.

"Almost there," Adam called out from the front.

Jade found herself getting more excited. This was a crazy plan but it just might work. There was no way that Zak would ever expect them to hide out in his house.

"Park in the drive," Cole ordered. "You and I will get out and walk right up to the front and knock. If any of his neighbours are around they won't find that suspicious."

"He's got to have an alarm," she warned them.

Mitch nodded. "Yes, but we have Brady."

"What does that mean?" she asked.

"Brady knows the code," Mitch supplied.

"What?" she and Cole both said.

"I had to pick up his bag after a job one time. If he hasn't changed it, I should be able to get us in," Brady said quietly.

"Oh, this is perfect," Cole stated as he rubbed his hands together in glee. "Okay, Brady, you're with me and Adam. Mitch and Jade, stay in the van in case someone is there."

The vehicle slowed so she turned to look out of the dark window. They were in a very nice neighbourhood with clean streets, green lawns and very little activity. Halfway down the block, Adam pulled into a short drive.

She was a little surprised at how beautiful the outside was. For some reason she hadn't seen the huge tiger shifter doing yard work and maintaining a house on the weekends. "I love the landscape. I'll have to ask him who he uses."

"Zak did most of the work himself. He's still playing around a little but he has put a lot of work into his home. Even more so when he started up with Abilene," Brady told them.

Jade was impressed. Her own small house needed lots of work but she'd only been there for six months and hadn't decided what she wanted to do yet. She planned to stay in Lake Worth, that was for sure, and whether it was with the FBI or the Coalition, she wanted to put down some roots.

"Okay, we do this quickly but quietly. We need to secure the property and see if it'll work to bring Luca back," Cole stated. "Let's do this."

Cole and Brady opened the back door as Adam climbed out of the front. With the doors closed, Jade could only watch as the three men made their way up the sidewalk. It was times like these that she wished she had Cole's hearing.

"Do you hear anything?" she asked Mitch.

Mitch shook his head. "No, it's quiet."

A comfortable silence settled in the van as they waited to find out if this would be a successful stop or not. The longer the three shifters were gone, the more nervous she grew.

"So how'd you end up getting partnered with Cole?" Mitch broke the quiet.

She glanced over at him. He leant forward with his forearms braced on his knees, watching her. She shrugged. "I transferred here about six months ago. Cole didn't have a partner so I took the position," she answered. Of course, she left out all the shit that Cole had had to deal with. His old partner refusing to work with a shifter. No one else willing to take his place.

"Did you know right away what he is?" Mitch questioned.

"Sure," she said. "I knew some people had issues but I had already started my research on comparing the shifter traits opposed to fully human ones. I wanted to find out how we can use the shifter gene in the field and hopefully keep agents safer."

"Cole was research? I bet he loved that."

"No," she laughed. "He wouldn't have allowed that. My research showed that I accepted the shifter agents and the agency wanted to partner up a shifter with a human."

"I bet that went over well," Mitch stated sarcastically.

"Yeah, I lost a lot of friends with that, but it's true. I've learned more from Cole than any other agent. He has no problem with humans or shifters. If they are decent to him, he respects them. It's the humans in charge that are causing the problems we're having. When the boss isn't supporting the shifter agents, the field agents know they can get away with it too. It's wrong and I want to help people see that," she explained.

"Why? Most of the human agents wouldn't bother," Mitch pointed out.

"I know. I had a shifter save my life once. It was before I was here but still… I just feel like I should help others like him," she said. Jade didn't really want to get into her past and how she'd first learned about the ability of some humans to transform. It was still painful. "I joined the FBI to help others. Now I find myself having to explain why we should work together."

"I haven't heard very good things about the FBI and how they treat their shifter agents. I was surprised when they asked to join the task force," Mitch told her.

"I was too," she admitted. "I put Cole's and my name down before even asking him. I think it's a great idea."

"They're coming back," he said.

She turned her head and saw that Mitch was right. Cole led Adam and Brady towards the van. She waited until they were all settled back inside. "Well?"

"This is going to be awesome," Cole told her.

"We're really going to do this?" she questioned. "I mean really?"

"Oh yeah," Adam said from the front.

Even Brady was nodding. "This is gonna work. They'll never expect it."

"Fine, but remember I'm human, so you'd better keep me from getting mauled," she told them.

Everyone laughed. Jade could admit that she really thought the plan was smart. She would never have thought of going to one of the agents' houses to hide out. She wouldn't have had the balls to suggest it. But there was no way that the ATF and Coalition agents would expect this move. Now came the hard part, though. They had to get Luca away from the others.

"There's a shopping centre a couple of of blocks over. Let's drive over there and talk out the next part. We need to get moving," Cole ordered.

"Got it," Adam said before starting the van.

Cole moved to the middle of the van to sit as he pulled out blueprints of the target house and his notebook. Mitch dropped down beside him before yanking out the bags that had been stashed inside. All their equipment was packed inside the duffel bags.

When Adam rolled to a stop he shut off the vehicle before joining them in the back.

"Brady, were you able to overhear anything before we left?" Adam asked.

"What do you mean?" Cole asked.

"While I was waiting for us to leave I might have hung around the hall where the others were planning," Brady shared.

"You did?" Jade questioned, impressed.

"People don't notice me. I hang around and they just overlook that I'm there," Brady said. "It comes in handy."

"That's awesome," Jade complimented.

"They have three mission points to accomplish," Brady began. "They have to hide Luca. Also, a box is coming into the bus station that needs to be picked up and secured. Last, once they secure the package, Luca will give them coordinates to drop it off. If they get to the location and deliver the parcel while keeping Luca, they win."

"So if we get Luca, they don't get the location and we have their hostage," Jade supplied. "They're screwed."

"And they'll never find us at Zak's," Cole said.

She was really starting to get excited. This was their first training exercise with the joint task force and if they could pull this off the other agents would have to admit that she and Cole had something to add.

"From what I gathered, Zak and Jamie are going for the package with a few others. If we can get to Luca before they return, we'll have a much better chance," Brady said.

"So we go now," Cole stated. "They won't know what hit them."

"How are we going to get close without being spotted?" Jade asked. "The birds will see us coming if we try to sneak in the back."

"We're fast," Adam added. "But she's right. They have a cheetah shifter. If they get the warning, we won't be able to take him. As soon as they see the van they'll know it's us."

"So we don't use the van," Cole replied.

Jade knew that look on her partner's face. It was the same as when they were about to hit a house serving a warrant. He had a plan.

"You want to use our SUV?" she guessed.

"Yes," he agreed.

"They'll still see us coming. If we split up and take the front and back, there's a good chance one of the birds will spot us," Brady pointed out.

"We're not going to split up and we're not going to sneak in," Cole told them. "We're going to hit fast and hard."

Jade, along with the rest of the team, stared at Cole in shock. Cole grinned back. "Come on, they'll not know what hit them until it's too late."

She had to give her partner credit. Cole's plan was bold. If they could get to Luca before the other team was there, they had it made. "It's worth a shot," she said.

"That's the spirit." Cole grabbed her shoulder. "We'll surprise them and be gone by the time Zak and Jamie return. Afterwards we'll split up and swap vehicles. Adam, Mitch and you will take Luca back to Zak's in the van, while me and Brady drive the SUV around for a while. We'll make tracks to the Coalition office first before heading to the FBI building. There we'll switch out our SUV for another one," he told Jade.

Jade nodded. "Let's do this."

"Okay, let's get our equipment on and get ready to move quickly. We'll grab our vehicle from the office. Adam, you and Mitch stay with the van and follow us to the drop-off point. From there we'll all pile into the SUV and go."

The exhilaration coursing through Jade made it hard to remain seated. She was ready to go.

Chapter Four

Luca relaxed into the couch at their hideout as Zak, Jamie and Abilene prepared to leave. The first stage of the mission was to pick up a box from the bus station that needed to be taken to another location.

Only Luca knew where the package would have to be delivered, but he couldn't tell the team until they returned with it. Luca was playing the hostage and was already having fun with his friends. Even when Jamie had suggested tying him up. Luca knew that the others would never allow that. He did promise not to attempt escape, though. The training exercise was designed to use all their skills and he didn't see the ATF and Coalition failing.

Even with Sam and Patrick, the human agents, they had a better chance of completing the mission than the unit they were up against. Luca had to credit Cole and Jade with intelligence and passion for the work, but he was certain that they would fail. He'd been working with the Coalition for a while now and they were the best agents he'd had the pleasure of watching. They used their shifter senses so seamlessly that even he was learning more about his animal side. Which was one of the reasons he'd been considering a transfer. By having the Coalition, all of the shifters got to hone their skills in both human and shifter form. Luca wanted to soak up as much as he could from the others. Cole and Jade just didn't have the same experience.

Not that he would mind spending more time with Jade. He'd enjoyed talking with her the day before and the questions she'd asked about the previous missions had shown him that she was truly interested in the joint task force. She wanted to help the FBI shifter agents. He was curious in finding out more about why.

"So you think you'll get rescued?" Ryder asked him as he joined Luca on the couch. Ryder was part of Cody's birds of prey division. Luca really liked the young agent, even if he was a little scary when it came to hand-to-hand battle. Ryder was dangerous, so Luca was glad that they were on the same side.

"Not really," he admitted. "What about everyone else?"

"They don't seem too worried. They're taking off now to go collect the package. When they get back we'll drop it off and have two points done. All we'll have left is keeping you close," Ryder informed him.

"Are they taking the two FBI agents?" Luca asked. He hoped so. Unlike Cole and Jade, whom Luca didn't mind, working with the feebies that had joined them just that morning was already getting on his nerves. The two humans kept to themselves and didn't speak with any of them. They appeared to be just as bigoted as Luca had heard the rest of the FBI could be. If Cole and Jade surprised all of them, these other two didn't.

"They're leaving one with us and taking the other," Ryder said.

Luca hoped that by separating the two he might actually find out that they were all right guys.

"I'm going to shift and keep watch on the roof," Ryder told him. "Don't get taken on purpose. No matter how hot you think the Fed is."

Luca had to laugh at Ryder's comment. It wasn't really a surprise that people had picked up on his attraction to Jade. Abilene hadn't managed to get him alone, but Luca knew that as soon as she did he was in for a lecture from his partner. *Like he needed it.* He was fully aware that Jade was human and worked for an organisation that didn't allow mating between humans and shifters. If he wasn't careful she'd call his brother, and Sal would love to stick his nose into Luca's business. "Just be careful," Luca replied.

Ryder walked off, leaving him alone in the living room. The house that they were using was one of the Coalition's safe locations. According to the rules of the mission the other team already knew his location. They would come for him. He didn't know if they knew about the package. Maybe they would go that route. Try to get both him and the parcel. That would be bold. *And stupid.* He'd be disappointed if they attempted both. There was no point in taking on more than they needed. The only reason to go after the box would be pride. But the feebies were arrogant so maybe they would try.

"We're taking off," Zak called from the doorway. "We'll be back in less than two hours. Be ready to move then."

Luca nodded. "You got enough men staying?"

"You're covered. We're split in half. I don't expect them to go after the package, but you never know. We lose it, or you, and we're screwed," Zak replied.

Luca stood and walked over to his friend. "Stay safe."

Zak grinned. "I'm just ready for the fun to begin. I know how the wolves work. The Fed might surprise me."

He knew that Zak was loving this. Luca motioned to his partner waiting by the front door. "Keep her out of trouble."

"But that's how I like her," Zak said. He winked at Luca before strolling away.

Luca laughed, shaking his head. The door closed behind the agents as they left. Glancing over, he noticed the human feebie watching him closely.

"Hey, man," Luca called out. "Want to join me for a cup of coffee?" he asked Sam.

Sam looked undecided for several seconds before finally nodding. Luca waved for Sam to follow him into the kitchen. Luckily the house was already stocked with a few supplies, which included coffee, creamer and sugar. Luca started a pot then turned to lean against the counter. Sam remained standing in the doorway.

"I don't bite," Luca said. "Well, not without permission—and only women."

Sam didn't even crack a smile at Luca's joke. He did move to an island bar stool and take a seat, though.

"So, I take it you didn't volunteer for this assignment?" Luca said.

Sam's head snapped up and he glared at Luca. "What's that supposed to mean?"

Luca shrugged. "It's obvious that you don't want to be here."

He surprised Luca by sighing. He started to shake his head. "It's not that, really. I know it seems like it, but we have a lot of pressure coming down from our boss."

"What kind of pressure?" Luca questioned.

"Just some…stuff. I don't want to get into it, but we're dealing with it."

Luca didn't like the answer, but he knew better than to push. He turned to pull down two mugs. "How do you take your coffee?" he asked. He went ahead and added a small amount of sugar to his own. He looked around when Sam didn't answer.

"I don't have a problem with shifters," Sam told him. He'd lifted his head to meet Luca's gaze. Luca believed him. It was weird, and he might end up being totally wrong, but he didn't get a bad feeling from Sam.

"Good to know," Luca said. "Coffee?"

"Black's fine," Sam replied.

He poured steamy coffee into the two cups before sliding one carefully across the counter.

"Thanks." Sam smiled as he picked up his beverage and blew on it.

Luca continued to watch him. He was average looking in his blue suit and tie. Nothing really stood out about him. He probably made a good Fed but Luca didn't get the same dedicated and intense feel as he did from Cole and Jade. Actually, Sam appeared the complete opposite of them. When Cole and Jade walked into a room they demanded attention—Cole with his alpha dominance and Jade with her warm, sweet allure.

They were a power couple of in the government and would go far if they didn't get mixed up in the shifter issues. Although, Luca didn't believe that Jade would be able to avoid it. She was spunky and obviously cared about her partner. Cole was a little harder to read. He didn't talk as much as Jade, and while Luca had been filling Jade in on all the previous training, Cole had just sat back and watched. They had a very interesting partnership. It was obvious in the way that Cole allowed her to speak for both of them that he respected her. Luca could see the tight connection between the two of them.

At least he didn't get the feeling that they were more than partners. Even if he decided not to act on the attraction between him and Jade, Luca really didn't want to have to go up against Cole. Cole was obviously more dominant. There was no doubt that if Cole was in a pack he'd be high up in rank.

Just because Cole was a wolf shifter didn't mean that he was with a pack, though. It was rare for wolves to be rogue or on their own, but if anyone could handle living without family it would be Cole.

Luca still considered himself part of his home pack even though he didn't live close to his family any longer. He made certain to return to his parents and siblings at least every three months. They would shift and run together under the moon. While the moon wasn't necessary to be able to transform, Luca's father had always loved to play around with the old legends.

He kind of liked it himself. When the shifters around the world had announced their presence, the entire Perez clan had gathered to decide whether they would join along. Luca and Sal had had no problem at the idea of being out in the open but their mom had been worried. She didn't want her kids to get hurt by humans who feared what they didn't understand. Luca had been lucky. His agency and friends had no problem with the shifter side of him. It was tougher for Sal, though. The FBI had actually suspended all shifters right after the announcement had been made. Both Sal and his partner were still fighting for their rights to be the same as their human counterparts.

"Did you know Special Agent Babcock or Adams before this?"

Sam's question drew him out of his own thoughts and back to the present. "Sorry, no, we met them yesterday morning."

"Oh, you guys just seemed to get along really well already," Sam said.

Luca wasn't sure how to explain why he was so comfortable with Cole and Jade. There was just something about them he liked.

"Is it because Agent Babcock is a shifter?" Sam asked.

"No, other than my partner, I'm used to working with humans at the ATF."

"So you're partnered with another shifter? Is that mandatory at your agency?" Sam questioned.

"We were already assigned to each other so it worked out well in the end," Luca shared.

"I lost my partner when he came out as a shifter," Sam told him.

Luca paused with his mug halfway to his mouth. Even at the ATF there had been a lot of partner exchanges when one found out about the other's shifter status. But it was a major issue at the FBI according to his brother. He had to wonder why someone who had abandoned his partner would accept a position on the joint task force. He was at a loss for words. "Were the two of you close?" he asked with caution.

"I thought so. I didn't take it well at first. I was a prick to him. I think now I was just shocked and listened to some of the assholes around the office. I'm hoping that I can make it up to him, though. Ask for his forgiveness," Sam stated. "I'm just not sure where to start."

Ah, so that was why Sam wanted to talk to him. Get some advice. Luca didn't mind if it would help Sam's partner. "Are you still both assigned to the same division?"

"No. After the FBI was required to take the shifters back, they were all moved into one unit. Until I met Agents Babcock and Adams I didn't know that any team was combined shifter and human. My boss told me it was against regulation when I enquired about getting Danny back."

It was such a shame that, even in the government, shifters weren't getting the same rights as other workers. Luca was happy to be part of the unit trying to protect shifters' rights and make sure that they were treated as equals. "What does he do now?"

"Fieldwork," Sam replied. "I'm not sure what, exactly. They don't come onto our floor, and we have a separate locker room and gym they're not allowed to use."

Luca saw red as anger filled him. That was such bullshit. No one deserved to be treated that way. He took several deep breaths before he could speak again. By the time his vision had cleared, Sam had his head bent over his cup, frowning.

"Sorry, man, but your division is fucked up. I've not heard that things were that bad for the shifters."

"I don't think it's everywhere. I've tried to discreetly ask around to some guys I was in the academy with, but they didn't really want to talk to me about it. I think they're afraid to take a side in the matter."

Someone needed to. If the shifters were being mistreated like Luca suspected they were, someone needed to step in. If it had to be Luca then so be it. He'd get hold of his brother and hopefully, with the help of Cole and Jade, they'd all figure out how to help. "What kind of shifter is your partner, uh, did you say Danny?"

"Danny O'Brien," Sam said. "And I don't actually know." Sam flushed in obvious embarrassment.

Yeah, Sam must have turned his back on his partner quickly if he didn't even know what kind of shifter the man was. But at least he was trying to do the right thing now. "How does your new partner feel about all this?"

Sam looked over his shoulder as though he expected Patrick to be standing right behind him, listening. "Pat's got a few things of his own he needs to take care of. Some mistakes he made. That's not my story to tell, though."

"Do you think he'd be interested in joining in if I could come up with a plan to help the shifters in your office?" Luca asked, leaning closer to Sam. He didn't want to promise anything too big, but there was no way now that he'd heard about Sam and his partner's problems he could just let it go.

"What?" Sam jumped to his feet. "No, man, I thought… I mean, I didn't want… You can't get involved."

Luca didn't miss the way Sam's hands shook before he stuffed them in the front pockets of his suit. "Hey, it's okay, I just want to help. It sounds like the bosses might be up to no good. I just want to make sure everyone's safe." Sam was obviously worried about his ex-partner and Luca hoped he could get through to the young agent. "To make sure Danny isn't being used or hurt."

"I—" Sam frowned as he started to back off. "I gotta take a piss."

Luca allowed him to leave, hoping that Sam could see that he just wanted to help. Luca didn't know where the other agents were in the house. Ryder had gone outside and he suspected that some of the others were also spread out keeping watch. He picked up his cup and strolled to the glass door that opened into the front of the house. Just one of the two entrances that faced the street.

They didn't have safe houses like this at the ATF. The Coalition not only had more money but was better supplied than the older government agency. Luca was just a little jealous. This home base was nicer than the apartment he was currently renting.

He missed his family even though he was surrounded by such good people that were quickly becoming his second family. He was renting two apartments—one there in Lake Worth, and the other his permanent address when located at the ATF. Neither was somewhere that he could see himself living in the next few years. He wanted to get his own house set up, but since his career was still up in the air, he was hesitant to do more than just lease a small space for now.

He'd been thinking about leaving the ATF to apply for the Coalition. It'd been pure luck that his last undercover assignment had landed him side by side with Zak. He wanted to transfer — the two things that kept him with his agency were his partner and the fact that he really did love what he did. The joint task force between the two organisations really was a dream come true. He and Abilene had to travel back to their office twice a week unless they were on a current case, but he didn't mind.

If the trial run worked, maybe he'd be able to buy a house like the one he was currently hiding in. Maybe even choose a fixer-upper like Zak had. That way he could custom repair it and have everything perfect. He'd need guest rooms for when his family visited, especially Sal, so an older structure might be better so he could afford to remodel.

In the reflection of the glass he could see his own smile. He tried to keep his excitement down but he'd have been lying to himself if he didn't admit how important it was that this task force worked.

The sound of a vehicle revving up pulled him from his thoughts. He gasped, spotting a huge SUV barrelling down the street and hopping the kerb.

A screech from Ryder above was his only warning before the vehicle stopped only yards from the door he was standing in front of.

Pop. Pop. Pop.

The SUV's doors flew open as the blast of their rounds hit the house. It was a good thing that they weren't using real bullets.

Ryder landed hard on the ground outside right before his eyes. He took a step back only to halt when he spotted Jade and Mitch glaring back at him through the door.

Luca's instructions were clear. He wasn't supposed to resist rescue even though that was what his instincts demanded he do. Mitch reached for the door only to find it locked. Jade grinned before using the butt of her rifle to smash the glass. The glee in her eyes was sexy as hell. Luca looked away so that his attraction wouldn't be obvious. Right in the middle of a mission was not the time to have the hots for a fellow agent.

Mitch made it through the door and grabbed him.

"Freeze!"

Oh thank God. Luca heard Sam's command and smiled back at the human agent. It wasn't going to be so easy to get him as they'd thought. Although really he was shocked that they'd been so bold as to hit the house with such extreme measures. No one had expected that.

"Move it. We're out of time." Cole's yell echoed around the quiet kitchen.

"Luca, move towards me," Sam ordered. "I have you covered."

Pop. Pop.

He ducked in reflex as another few rounds exploded. Jade strolled right up to Luca and grabbed his arm. She'd taken out Sam with her plastic bullets before anyone had moved. For a human, she moved quickly.

"We're here to save you, Mr. Perez. Please come with us," Jade said to him.

He nodded and allowed her to lead him from the broken kitchen glass door. The others in the rescue team were spread out through the yard covering him, Jade and Mitch. "Nicely done," Luca said as he passed Cole.

Cole only grinned back.

He was shoved none too gently into the back cargo area of the SUV. It was a tight fit, especially when Jade climbed in next to him. Crap, were they going to ride the entire way back to the Coalition like this? He started to pray that he'd be able to contain his arousal. Jade wouldn't pick up on it with only her human senses, but the shifters with him sure would.

Damn, what a time to be in close quarters with a beautiful woman. He'd have laughed if he wasn't trying so hard to will his cock to go down.

"Are you injured?" Jade's hand landed on his thigh as she checked him.

Luca managed, hopefully, to turn enough so that she didn't spot his erection. Her warm palm on him felt damn good. "I'm okay," he croaked out.

Chapter Five

It hadn't been the plan for Jade to end up in the back of the SUV with Luca, but she wasn't complaining. Cole had pushed her right behind him so she had that as her excuse to take in Luca's warm body and sexy citrus scent.

She might not have a nose like her partner but Luca smelt wonderful. She really wished that they were alone so that she could snuggle up close.

"You're sure you didn't get cut by any glass?" she asked, just to have a reason to talk to him.

"I'm sure," he promised.

Jade left her hand on his leg while she leant closer. Luca's hard muscles moved under her palm as he shifted around. It wasn't comfortable to be all bunched up. Although she did notice that he wasn't pushing her away. She also was aware of how stiff he held his body and that his breathing was heavier than it should have been. The walk to the SUV had been brisk but they hadn't been running. She peered at Luca's face trying to figure out if he was hurt and just not telling her. "If we hurt—"

"Jeez," he muttered.

"What?" she whispered back. She sat between his two outstretched legs, but in the dark vehicle she couldn't really see anything. She slid her hand up, checking for injuries. Luca groaned, and she froze.

"Trying to kill me?" he accused.

"What are you talking about?" she asked. Had he bumped his head? Why in the hell was he acting so weird? She glanced over the seat at the others to make sure that no one was watching. Adam was driving while Cole directed him from the passenger seat. Brady and Mitch were still discussing the quick rescue, retelling how they'd caught Ryder by surprise. Since everyone else's attention was elsewhere she went ahead and did what she wanted. She raised her free hand to Luca's shoulder and stroked while tightening her right on his leg. His body against hers felt just as good as she'd thought it would. His skin was hot and she loved the feel of his hard body.

Luca lifted his hips, making her hand brush over his lap and his, oh yeah, erection. He was turned on. She bit her bottom lip to keep herself quiet before deliberately running her hand back over his hard cock. He lurched up, grabbing her wrist to press her hand right up against his erection. "Stop teasing," he ordered in a low voice.

She shivered, turned on by his need. She brought her mouth a few inches from his. "I don't think you really want me to get you off when everyone in this vehicle would know," she murmured. "Do you?"

He bucked into her hold. "I'm trying to remember if I care or not."

She liked his admission. Still, as much as she'd love to show him how much she wanted him, she didn't want a quick feel in the back of a SUV with too many people close by. Tilting her head, she brushed her lips gently over his. His breath caught as she lifted her head before nodding.

"You're going to have to move your hand if you don't want me to embarrass myself," he whispered.

Jade sat back up, peering over the seat to make sure that everyone else was still occupied. Cole was looking back at her over his shoulder with a grin. She shook her head, knowing that she'd get teased later. Luca shifted around so he was more comfortable.

"I can't believe you all pulled it off," Luca told them.

Mitch laughed before reaching back to pat Luca's arm. "I had no doubt. It went perfectly."

"I don't know about that. Ryder fell pretty hard." Luca sounded worried.

"I checked on him," Cole said. "He was playing it up. He doesn't want his ass kicked by Zak when the others return."

Luca chuckled as if he could understand Ryder's dilemma. He caught Jade's gaze and nodded then turned to look out of the window. "This isn't the way to the Coalition," he said.

"We're not going back there," Jade replied.

"Really?" Luca asked. Was that approval on his face? "That's where they expect you to go."

"We know," she stated simply.

"This just gets better and better," Luca complimented. "So, where to?"

"Sorry, you may be working for the other side. We can't disclose our destination until you get a thorough pat down. We have to make sure you're not rigged with any listening devices or a way to contact the others," Jade said.

"You don't trust me?" The way that Luca batted his eyelashes did not fool Jade at all.

"No," she responded. "But don't worry. I'll make sure I'm the one that checks you over."

"Now I wish I'd planted something just to see how well you'll do."

She brushed her fingers over his arm before leaning closer. "I'm very dedicated to your safety, Mr. Perez," she stated, falling back into her role of agent and rescuer.

"I'm glad," Luca told her.

Jade knew that they weren't very far from where they'd hidden the other van. She grabbed hold of the seat in front of her just as the SUV slid to a stop. Luca, not knowing to brace himself, fell into her.

She was really enjoying this operation.

"Let's go, kiddies," Cole called.

Jade popped the back hatch open and climbed out. Once on solid ground she could stretch her legs. She reached to help Luca get out since it was harder for him as he was bigger than her.

She didn't let go when they were both free. Gripping his shoulder, she led him to the van. She opened the back door while motioning for Luca to sit down. Jade followed him in, making sure to remain close.

"You know the plan. Stick with it. If anyone has any problems or sees anything suspicious, call. We'll be back there in half an hour," Cole said.

"Got it," she answered just before Cole slammed the door closed. She turned to Luca. She hadn't been kidding about checking him over to make sure that the other team hadn't put a tracker or anything on him. "Do you want me to check you over or are you just going to hand me whatever device they have on you?" she asked sweetly.

Luca laughed. "I have no idea what you mean."

"Have it your way," she told him. Standing, she pulled him up with her. As much as she would have loved to tease him a little more, she did have a job to do. She ran her hands down his neck to his shoulders, arms and hands. Crouching, she also checked his boots, legs and waist.

Luca moved side to side, and the evidence that he was enjoying her manhandling of him was obvious. His erection was so close to her face that she could have leant forward a little and touched it with her mouth.

"Like this?" she taunted.

Luca nodded. "More than you know. I was attracted to you right from the start, but seeing you tonight in action — wow."

She hummed, pleased with his admission. "Maybe if you're a good boy I'll..." Jade pulled a small silver locator chip from Luca's belt. "Gotcha!"

He groaned. "I didn't think you'd find it."

"We're a lot better than you think," she told him.

"I didn't mean it as an insult. That was the best place I could think to hide it," he said sincerely. He cupped her face, pulling her up to stand in front of him. "I'm serious, I admire you and your partner. You've got skills and really showed them off. It couldn't have been easy to work with new team members for the first time and pull all this off."

Staring into his dark eyes, Jade felt just a little lost. She hadn't even known this man for forty-eight hours but she felt a deep connection already. She wondered if that was how other shifter and human relationships started. If the romantic feelings were causing her to become comfortable around him. But the problem with that reasoning was that she'd felt the same sense of ease around Cole the first time they'd met. Even the other shifters at the Coalition. There was just more to the level of contentment she felt around Luca.

Part of her experience with shifters was her research, and all the time she'd spent learning about them she'd never come across anyone else claiming an instant connection. It was all so confusing. Not that it really mattered when Luca started to lean forward.

She wanted him to kiss her. What did it matter why she was so in need of Luca Perez? She just was. Rising onto the tips of her toes, she met his mouth and sealed their lips together.

She jolted with arousal at the first gentle touch. Luca brought his arm around her waist to hold her tight as she opened for him. She moaned as their tongues brushed and she got her first real taste of him.

Jade gripped the front of his shirt, giving in to her desire to surrender to him.

The back door opened and they jumped apart quickly. She didn't miss Cole's amused smile. "Find anything?" he asked.

Pumped up with arousal and need, she was shaking, but she tossed the small chip to Cole. He caught it easily.

Cole glanced between the two of them, and Jade tried not to blush. With her partner's enhanced senses there were no doubt that he could smell the arousal from her and Luca. She refused to be embarrassed, though. The attraction was natural and she believed Luca to be a good guy. Cole would have to learn to accept him if things progressed further between her and Luca. Luckily Cole didn't comment on what he had to have suspected was going on. Instead he merely nodded. "Let's go then."

Jade backed away from Luca to take a seat on the bench. "You'll probably want to sit."

Luca nodded, taking the space across from her as the two front doors opened. Adam started the SUV before glancing over his shoulder at them. "I'll be your chauffeur tonight. Please keep your hands and feet inside the van at all times. Our destination's about ten minutes away."

"I think you're messing up your duties," Mitch commented.

"Where're Brady and Cole?" Luca questioned.

"They'll follow us. We decided that Adam and I would be the best ones for the next part of our plan," Mitch answered. "Just in case we're followed."

Jade nodded. They did need to get going so she didn't really care who drove them. "Let's hit it then."

Adam took off, and Jade and Luca jerked in the back, almost falling to the floor. "Oh yeah, make sure you hang on tight," he called to them.

She cursed quietly as Adam cackled from the driver's seat. He was crazy but she liked him. Adam actually reminded her of an old friend she'd grown up with.

The drive to Zak's house was mostly silent as everyone prepared for the next phase. Luca didn't ask any questions, which was good since no one would have answered him. As soon as Adam pulled into the driveway, Luca moved to peer out of the front windshield.

"You've got to be kidding!" Luca exclaimed.

Adam and Mitch started to laugh. Luca looked over at her. "He's going to kill you."

She shrugged. "He has to find us first."

"Oh, this is going to be so good." Luca sounded just as excited as her team. "I can't wait to see his face."

"Hurry up before someone sees us," Mitch ordered while opening his door.

Jade climbed to the back door, yanking on the lever to let them out. She went first and as soon as Luca dropped down beside her she put her hand on his shoulder.

"I don't think he's going to run," Adam told her.

"Can't take any chances. If we lose Luca then we have to deal with Cole. I'm more scared of Cole than Zak," she explained. And maybe she was pushing her job a little but she just wanted to be close to Luca. Who could blame her, really? But she did release her hold on him. He really wasn't trying to escape and she needed to get her head in the game. She could worry about what was going on between them later. She had a training exercise to win first.

"Let's go," Mitch whispered from the front of the van.

They trooped to the front door. Adam pulled the key from his front pocket. He went straight to the alarm pad and punched in four numbers. Once inside, no one turned on any lights.

"Hang onto me," Luca murmured. "I know my way around and I won't let you walk into anything."

Well, she wasn't going to argue with him. She slipped her hand into his as he led her through what she guessed was a hall.

"If we go back to the living room we can turn on the lights and no one will see if we use the lamps," Luca suggested. He strolled along the carpet, obviously knowing where he was going. Plus, he wouldn't be as blind as she since most shifters had extremely good eyesight from their shifter genes. Jade trusted him to keep his word and not let her bump into any furniture or walls.

"Here we go."

Luca switched on the lamp next to the couch. Jade looked around her at the spacious and warm room. There were several pictures up on the wall and resting on the mantle. The furniture looked masculine but comfortable. She liked the feel of the space. "This is nice," she commented.

"From what I understand, this place was a mess when Zak first bought it. He used his nights and weekends to slowly do all the remodeling and updating himself, with the help of his friends, of course," Luca said.

"I'm going to check out the rest of the place again," Mitch said. "Just to make sure there are no surprises waiting, but I think we should stay in here. There's playing a joke and then there's suicide. I don't want Zak to kill us."

"I agree," Jade replied.

"I can't believe you all thought of this. It's perfect. They'll never think of looking for you at their own home," Luca told her.

She still had her hand in his so she pulled him to the couch. "It's a little evil but brilliant."

Luca nodded. "So what now?"

"We sit and wait until time is up," she returned.

"Okay," Luca said. "There's something I wanted to talk to you and your partner about."

"What's that?" She turned on the couch so she was angled to see his face. She liked looking at him.

"I was talking with the other FBI agent, Sam, and from what I gathered things aren't going real well with the shifters at his division," Luca said. "I'm concerned they're being mistreated."

She sighed. She shared Luca's fear. But there wasn't much she could do about it. She could barely protect Cole from the haters. What could she do for other shifters? "I know," she admitted. "I just don't know what to do about it."

"It's a good thing you're with the Coalition," Luca said, smiling at her. "This is what we do."

"I don't see how you can do anything. It's a different agency." *But wouldn't it be great if Luca could help the shifters?*

"I have an idea," he said. "I want to talk to the others and Sam again before I take it to Commander Green, but I'm certain we'll figure it out."

Jade grew excited. It was so worth putting her career with the joint task force on hold if the shifters could get the help they needed. "I'll do whatever I can."

"What about your partner? Would he be willing to help?" Luca questioned.

"I'm sure he would. He refuses to bow down to anyone treating him like shit, but his hands are tied too. He barely kept his job and was transferred to be partnered with me. It's not been easy."

Mitch entered the living room with some bottles of water. "What's up? You two look serious," he commented.

"I have an idea," Luca said.

Jade listened to him fill Mitch in on his concerns and what he wanted. When Cole and Brady returned he went over it once again. He was passionate about the subject. Jade loved how his dark eyes lit up as he spoke.

"How are we going to find out where Sam's old partner is?" Cole asked. He sat across from Luca and Jade in one of the recliners. Jade knew her partner would be up for the mission and was happy to see that he seemed to share Luca's desire to do something.

"I have an inside man who would be willing to look into the subject discreetly," Luca informed them.

"Who?" Cole questioned.

"My brother."

"Your brother?" Jade repeated.

"He's a special agent in California. He works intelligence gathering so he should have access to the records we need. If not, he would know who does," Luca explained.

Jade was shocked. She'd had no idea that Luca's brother was a Fed. No wonder he had accepted her and Cole into the fold so easily. He had inside knowledge that not everyone in the FBI acted like assholes.

"I'd like to speak with him," Cole said.

"That can be arranged," Luca said. "I'd like to get a jump on this, though. If Sam's right, we need to move quickly."

"You think the others will share your concerns?" Cole asked.

"Oh yeah. Cody, Zak and Jamie will have our backs. And they're good investigators," Luca assured him.

"Do you think you'll be able to pull up anything from the files you have access to?" Cole asked Jade.

"What files?" Luca questioned.

"Because of my work in shifter behaviors, I'm copied in on reports from the field. I haven't had a lot of time to look through them, though. Right now I'm concentrating on how we can train our agents, shifter or human, from the beginning, so we can utilise all the gifts we have access to," she explained.

"That's great," Luca exclaimed. "If you can look into anything that seems off we can start our investigation there."

"Let me grab my laptop and I'll get started. Maybe there's something there we can share with the others when this exercise is over. It's not like we'll do much waiting to see if they find us."

Luca grinned. "I can guarantee they won't be looking for me here." He turned to Cole. "You like to live dangerously, my friend. It probably wasn't your idea, but you are in charge of this team."

Cole shrugged. "I have no problem taking the blame. I already like Zak and he might be pissed off but he'll appreciate our effort."

"Yeah, he will," Luca agreed. "Although, Jamie really is going to love this."

"I haven't made my mind up about him yet," Cole admitted. "I watched the tapes so I've seen him in action, but just talking to the guy—he's hard to take seriously."

"I know." Luca nodded. "But having him on your side is a good thing. When he's working he's completely dedicated to the mission. I've learned a lot from him. Although, when Abilene met Jamie she wanted to strangle him in the first five minutes."

"Really?"

Luca settled back on the couch. "My cover was blown and Zak had to either expose himself or find a way to get me out alive. He'd been ordered to kill me."

"Wow," Cole whistled.

"We faked a fight and at the end of it he shot me," Luca explained.

"Zak shot you?" Jade asked as she rejoined them. "No way."

Luca rolled his shoulder. There were a few times when his old wound still bothered him. Shifters healed quickly due to the fact that they could transform and rearrange their bodies, but they could also be killed easily. It didn't take a silver bullet either.

A lead one worked just as well. "It was the only way for me to get out. Zak made it appear that he'd killed me. After, I was able to make it to Abilene at a hotel. Jamie and Cody just happened to be there since she was doing a run on Zak and was growing suspicious."

"They were there when you showed up?" Cole asked. "That's some really good timing."

"It was," Luca acknowledged. "Abilene was pissed and wanted to go after Zak. Cody remained calm and did his best to defuse the situation, but Jamie, being Jamie, taunted her. From the little I remember she about took off his head."

"I would have loved to have seen that," Jade commented. She settled back on the couch next to him. Luca had to resist moving closer to feel her heat.

"Yeah, they're pretty tight now, but at the time I didn't think Jamie and Abilene would ever get along. The next day we combined forces and took the SIP down."

"SIP?" Jade asked looking up from her laptop.

"They call themselves Shifters in Power," Luca informed them.

"That's the case Cody's trying to wrap up?" Cole questioned.

"Yes, we got most of the members involved. Of course, some got away but they're in such deep hiding they shouldn't be able to cause too much trouble.

"That's good," Jade commented. She bent back over her computer.

"I haven't been working with the Coalition long but I've come to really admire them. They'll do everything in their power to help the agents with the FBI," he told Cole, lowering his voice so that he wouldn't bother Jade as they spoke.

"We're in," Cole told him. "I want to protect the others in my office. Some are even too scared to come out as shifters and they shouldn't be. I chose not to hide because I believe that if people know what I can do I'll be able to help more people."

"Commander Green will also be on our side. I should probably inform my boss what's going on but I want to talk to the others first. Maybe get the commander to call him."

"That would probably be best. The commander seemed like a take-charge kind of guy. You're sure your brother can help?" Cole asked.

"This is right up his alley," Luca said. "If there *is* anything going on here that's a threat to the shifters he'll want to be involved. Both he and his partner are shifters working in the FBI. They have a stake in this too."

"What can you tell me about Sam? I hadn't met him or Patrick before this and I'm getting an uneasy feeling about them."

"Sam seems to be worried. He also feels guilty because he didn't have his partner's back and basically abandoned him," Luca replied. "He doesn't trust us, either. It'll be hard but I think he'll do the right thing."

"We'll keep an eye on both of them. Maybe if I talk to Sam he'll respond to me being a shifter and a Fed?" Cole suggested.

Luca shrugged. "They might be helpful, though. We'll start with your office and see what we learn but we should search for his ex-partner too."

Jade grunted. "I think we'll have plenty to look into," she said.

"What did you find?" Cole asked. He leant forward in his chair. Luca moved closer to her too.

"I don't know yet," she said. She never took her eyes off her screen, though. "Some of these reports are incomplete. I can probably find the originals." She finally glanced up.

"Can I—" Cole began.

"I just got started." She pointed at Cole. "Don't rush me. You know I work better doing it myself anyway."

Cole laughed. "I know."

She huffed. "I'm going to make some coffee."

She stood and carried her laptop with her. Luca peered over at Cole.

"She gets like this when she finds something interesting. We'll see her in a couple of of hours. It drives me crazy at the office but Jade is the best at piecing together information that other people would miss," Cole explained to Luca.

Luca grinned. "I guess we wait. I wonder what Zak's doing now."

Both he and Cole laughed at that.

Chapter Six

It was all Luca could do not to laugh as Zak stormed into his own living room. He was still on the couch relaxing and speaking with Cole. Jade had moved to the kitchen table to work on getting him some files about the shifters in her office, and Mitch, Brady and Adam were out front with the members of Zak's team that had shown up.

Cody had called to get the address where they were holed up once the time limit had passed. Cole's team had won. As soon as Mitch had given Cody Zak's street address, Zak had started to curse.

"You broke into my house," Zak accused, glaring at Cole.

"Technically we didn't. Brady had the alarm code and knew where the spare key was," Cole corrected.

"I'll kill him," Zak threatened.

"Come on, man. This is epic!" Jamie said as he bounced in. He was followed by Cody and Abilene.

Zak spun around and pointed at Jamie. "Don't start."

Jamie laughed at him. Zak jumped forward, but Abilene slid between the bear shifter and her lover. "Hey." She cupped Zak's face. She waited until Zak had stopped glaring at Jamie and looked at her. Abilene smiled sweetly before kissing Zak with a gentle peck.

Luca couldn't believe how Zak calmed right before his eyes. The connection between Zak and Abilene reminded him of his parents. Abilene was able to settle Zak with just a small touch.

"Fine," Zak conceded. "I won't kill anyone."

"Good, because you know it's awesome. We've been chasing our tails all damn night and never even considered looking at our house," Abilene told him.

Zak growled before wrapping his arms around Abilene's waist. "You just called it our house," he pointed out.

Abilene shook her head. Since Abilene had starting staying with Zak she'd never admitted to actually moving in. Maybe this would be it. If she could just get over the final hurdle and commit to Zak, the two of them would be so happy.

Luca felt bad witnessing such an intimate moment but Zak and Abilene didn't seem to mind having an audience. Of course, Zak wasn't the type to care what anyone thought.

"Maybe I do think about it being our house, our home," Abilene whispered.

With a whoop, Zak lifted Abilene up into his arms while kissing her passionately.

"I don't think he cares about who broke in anymore," Jamie said, joining Luca on the couch.

"We didn't break in," Cole repeated.

Jamie waved his hand. "Whatever. I just know that next time we're on an exercise I'm on your team."

"Sounds good," Cole agreed.

Luca glanced back and forth between Jamie and Cole. He wouldn't have pegged them for becoming friends. Cole was very serious and pure dominant while Jamie acted like a clown at times. But Jamie was one of the best agents that Luca had ever worked with. Cole and Jamie would be a hard team to beat. "While all of you are in here there's something I want to talk to you about," Luca mentioned.

"Okay." Cody moved farther into the room. He'd been messaging on his phone and Luca doubted that it would have been to anyone other than his mate, Aubrey.

Zak dragged Abilene over to the other recliner, sitting and pulling her onto his lap.

Luca caught Cole's gaze. He felt as though he had the most support from the wolf shifter. Oh, he knew that Jade wanted to help but it was obvious that Cole had been keeping things from her. As soon as Jade had left the room, Cole had quickly filled him in on what was really going on. The threats and pranks the other agents were aiming at Cole. The bad mouthing, reports going missing, and late backup. Cole was worried but hadn't informed Jade yet. Cole nodded before leaning back in his chair. Guess it was up to Luca then.

"Here's what's up," Luca began.

He spoke calmly and only shared what he knew. While he had a lot of suspicions, he needed more information before he could accuse the FBI of abusing shifters.

Jamie was the first to speak up once he'd finished. "We need to talk to the commander."

"I agree, but we need more. Jade's trying to find the files on the shifters in her office. See if they're being sent on more dangerous missions without backup. I called Sal already. He's researching it at his end also."

"What do you suggest we do in the meantime?" Zak asked.

Luca felt bad about taking away the happy look on his face from earlier. Zak was frowning while he rubbed Abilene's back. Luca worried that the conversation would remind Zak about his past. Zak had been used by his own family. His dad and uncle hadn't cared what had happened to him as long as he'd got the job done. Very much like the shifters in the FBI.

"If you know anyone at all in the FBI we need to talk to them. Right now it's just the two offices but that can't be all. Sal's not mentioned any problems but I don't know that he would," Luca said.

"I think this is worth looking in to," Cody stated, standing. "We're supposed to have the day off for running a night session but we could meet up later?"

"Yeah, we all need some sleep," Luca admitted. "I'm exhausted."

"Why doesn't everyone take off and hit the sack?" Zak suggested. "It's just past seven now. We can meet back here about one and cook out and go through ideas. It will give us all time to think."

"You're offering your house?" Jamie questioned with suspicion.

Zak tightened his arm around Abilene's shoulders. "Our house, yes. It's not like anyone needs directions, right?"

Cole laughed as he stood. "You've been a good sport." He offered his hand to Zak.

Zak shook his hand. "Sure."

"Okay, I have a buddy I can call. I'll do that on the way home so hopefully he'll be able to get back to me before our meeting," Jamie said as he also stood.

Relief rushed through Luca and he was filled with admiration for the other agents. They were taking this seriously and wanted to help. He hadn't doubted it — well, he'd wondered if they'd think he should mind his own business — but they had his back.

"I'll check in with Jade. And tell her the plan." Luca rose.

"If anyone needs to crash here they can," Zak offered.

Everyone turned to him at the same time.

"What?" he snapped.

"Did you just invite guests?" Jamie questioned in a whisper.

"I'm being nice," Zak exclaimed.

"I know and it's scary," Jamie replied.

This time when Zak growled he showed Jamie his teeth.

"Jade and I are local so we can go home. I'll drop the other two Feds at their hotel so I don't think you'll have anyone who needs to bunk down here," Cole commented.

"If you take Sam and Patrick, I can drop off Jade," Luca said as innocently as he could manage.

Cole eyed him for a moment before nodding. Luca knew that Cole was aware of the attraction between him and Jade. He was just glad that Cole didn't say anything in front of the others. The display between him and Jade earlier hadn't been mentioned and Luca knew that he should have been more careful, but there was just something so special about Jade that he couldn't keep from thinking about how the two of them would be together.

Cole strolled to the front of the house while Luca went to the kitchen. He pushed the door open and wasn't surprised to see Jade hunched over her laptop typing away. She glanced up when she heard him.

"I think I've found some interesting reports. The good news is I have access to the personal files of the shifters, but it will take a while to sort through them," she told him.

"We're going to get some rest and meet back here at one. Cole is dropping off the other two Feds so I offered to take you home," Luca said.

Jade smiled. "Hmm."

He didn't know what she was thinking but the way she ran her gaze up and down his body had Luca hard instantly. She stretched her arms over her head, causing her back to pop. The move also made her shirt stretch up to reveal a patch of flawless tanned flesh. He crossed the room quickly until he towered over her. "What was that sound for?" he whispered.

"I wouldn't mind going to bed," she murmured. "Maybe with some company?"

Luca reached down to pull her to her feet. "That can be arranged," he stated before lowering his mouth to hers.

Jade kissed him back with the same amount of passion. There was no question that she wanted him as much as he did her. As their tongues twined and brushed together, he slid his hands down her back to cup her butt and lift her. She wrapped her legs around his waist, trusting him to be able to hold her. He didn't have a problem with her weight. Not that she would have been heavy for a human to carry. But with his shifter strength he could concentrate even more on her mouth and giving her pleasure.

As she ran her hands over his neck, Luca felt himself getting lost in her touch. He wanted to forget everything, just lay her back on the table and plunge inside her.

With a groan, he pulled back. "We should get out of here," he told her although he didn't let her go. Her face was flushed and her eyes were glazed over. She looked absolutely breathtaking.

"A bed would probably work better than your friend's kitchen table," she agreed.

Yes, they were definitely on the same page. "Let's get you packed up." He grabbed her bag from the floor and set it on the table while she closed down her computer. She handed him her laptop, which he placed in the free compartment. He noticed that some clothes were also inside. "A change of clothes?" he asked.

She grinned. "Never know when you're going to need them."

That worked out perfectly. He wouldn't even have to drive her back to her house at all. "My apartment is only a couple of blocks from here."

"Let's go," she responded as she slipped her bag over her shoulder.

Just as they reached the kitchen door it swung open.

Zak peered inside. "Everyone took off. Abilene is in the shower but she said to tell you to pick up some chips before you head back."

Luca nodded. "No problem. Anything else?"

"Nah, Jamie's going to grab the beer and Aubrey volunteered to grab some burgers and buns when Cody called her. We think she might be able to help with some of the off-the-records investigating," Zak informed him.

"Sounds good to me. Why don't you run up with Abilene? I'll lock the door behind me," he offered. If he knew his partner and Zak—they wouldn't just be going to bed for sleep.

Zak grinned. "Thanks, man."

Zak held the door open so that he and Jade could slip through. Zak parted company at the stairs, waving to them.

"I like how close everyone in the Coalition is," Jade commented.

It was one of the first things he'd also noticed about the others. "Yeah, Cody, Zak and Jamie all came from the same police department and joined at the same time so I can understand them being close, but they've welcomed all of us in," Luca said. He pulled open the door allowing Jade to exit first. He locked the knob before closing it behind him.

"From what I've gathered they don't work every case together, though?" she questioned.

"No, they do have their specialties and own teams. Cody was a homicide detective so he still handles that. He had the biggest unit. Jamie only has two other guys on the bear team and Zak works with a partner," he said.

"The commander allows them to work their strengths," Jade commented. "I liked him when we met."

"I do too," Luca agreed. "We've done a little work with each group but I'm closer to Zak. We were undercover together for a long time and became friends."

They reached his SUV, which Abilene had driven over after he'd been rescued. He clicked the key fob unlocking the doors before he opened hers. She placed her hand on his arm. "You want to remain with them, don't you?"

Luca met her gaze. She was insightful. He didn't know if it was from her experience as a behaviorist or if she could just read people. He wouldn't normally admit it to someone that he'd just met, but if he was going to be intimate with Jade then he needed to trust her. "I was already thinking about applying to the Coalition before my last mission. After I met Zak and found out he was part of this it just really cemented what I wanted. I didn't want to leave Abilene, though. We make good partners. The joint task force was perfect."

She leant up and brushed her lips over his. "We'll make it work. It will be the best combined unit in the country."

Wow! She was wonderful. He yanked her closer when she went to step back. He devoured her mouth, showing her what he had planned for later, and hoping that she understood his thanks.

Jade gave as good as he did. He ripped his mouth away, panting. "Thank God my apartment is close." He pushed her into the seat, before slamming the door closed and racing to his own side. Her soft laughter followed him.

He kept his eyes on the task at hand—getting the two of them safely to his place so he could get her naked. He was scared that if he even looked at her he wouldn't be able to resist pulling over on the side of the road and taking her right there. That wouldn't go over too well with his superiors.

He backed out of Zak's drive and onto the quiet residential street—now his partner's. He greedily thought about that instead of the sexy woman beside him. He was glad that Abilene was finally coming around to admitting to living with Zak. Not only did that leave the apartment free for him and Jade, but the admission had made Zak happy.

Taking the first right, he resisted the urge to speed.

He'd chosen a place not far from Zak because it was close to the Coalition also. They passed a couple of of blocks but he finally couldn't resist peering over at his passenger. Jade was watching him with a smirk. Okay, so she'd probably figured out what he was doing.

Her hand covered his thigh. Oh yeah, she knew. He took a deep breath and blew it out slowly. He was so hard. He couldn't remember the last time he'd wanted someone so badly.

He was damn relieved when he spotted his complex. He pressed his foot down to the gas pedal as Jade slid her hand from his leg to brush over his erection. He groaned while he lifted his hips slightly. "Almost there," he told her. Was that his voice? He sounded breathless and needy even to his own ears.

"Don't speed, Agent," she teased.

Fuck that. He took the next turn too sharply, causing the tires to squeal. Jade laughed before pressing down against his cock. Yeah, that was it. The feel of her hand was great. He wanted to feel it on his naked flesh, though. He could make it.

He slowed enough to enter the parking lot carefully. Jade squeezed him, and his eyes almost crossed. If he didn't get her inside he was going to come in his pants like a horny teenager. He saw the first spot in front of his house and parked. He turned off the SUV to quickly get out. He was around to Jade's side without her even reaching for the handle. He yanked the door open and pulled her into his arms. He didn't waste any time. He devoured her.

She tasted like coffee, cinnamon and vanilla. A flavour that he could become addicted to.

"Take me inside," she ordered while she gripped his shirt.

That was a much better idea than making out in public. He picked her up and turned.

"Wait," she cried out.

Luca stopped but frowned.

"My bag. And the door's open," she told him.

He wanted to stomp his feet in frustration but that probably wouldn't have been attractive. "Fine." He released her.

She ran over grabbed her bag. Once she'd slammed the door closed he gripped her hand and tugged her up the sidewalk.

The keys were in his hand so he rushed to get the door open. Once he was successful, he pushed her through and followed. Jade dropped her belongings, shoved him back against the closed door, and jumped him. Luca caught her easily.

"I love that. You'll never let me fall," she stated.

"Of course not," he agreed. It hadn't been a question but he wanted her to know that he would always catch her.

"Kiss me again. I love your mouth," she pleaded.

He planned to show her a lot more of it. He did as she'd requested. He slid his tongue between her lips. He swallowed her moan of pleasure. Turning, he switched their positions so that her back was anchored to the solid surface. He had to get his hands on her.

Luca started with her top. Jade licked down his neck and began yanking at his shirt before she pulled back.

"Naked," she demanded.

He stepped back and started to yank off his clothes. Jade went to unbuckle her pants but he slapped her hands away. "Mine," he told her.

She lifted an eyebrow. "Fine. Get to it then."

Luca took his time. He slowly revealed her, inch by inch. Each time he removed an article of clothing he peppered her skin with kisses. Even her feet when he pulled off her boots and socks. By the time he had her panties falling to the floor she was whimpering with need. It was music to his ears.

Jade was braced with her back to his front door so he spread her legs open wider, allowing him to run his fingers through her wet folds. She bucked into his palm but Luca was only just starting.

With his left hand he urged her to place her leg over his shoulder. This gave him even better access to her glistening pussy. He lowered his mouth and licked at her. She moaned, and he heard a thump from where he suspected her head had hit the wood. He didn't look up as he went back to licking her open.

He slid one finger inside her as he mouthed her clit. Her pussy tasted just as good as her mouth. He sniffed, taking in her scent along with her flavour. He loved sampling a woman's pussy and Jade's was unbelievable.

He continued to tease her, but his body was making it hard to concentrate. His cock was so hard and all he really wanted to do was bury himself inside her. But first he wanted to overwhelm her with pleasure.

Jade gripped his head while moving her hips to try to get more sensation. He added a second finger while he drew his mouth away.

"Luca," she called.

He pumped his fingers inside.

"Luca!"

They'd both been on the edge since the first time they'd been thrown together in the back of the SUV. He slid up her body and stood, keeping his digits deep in her. Lowering his mouth to her, Luca kissed her thoroughly.

Her nails scratched at his shoulders as she went crazy trapped between him and the door. It was a powerful feeling to have Jade at his mercy. He rubbed his erection across her leg, building up his own pleasure.

Jade ripped her mouth away. "In me now."

Chuckling, he removed his fingers and gripped her waist. "Hold onto me," he ordered.

Once she had a good grip on his shoulders he lifted her up. She wrapped her legs around him. Leaning her shoulders back to the door, he used his left hand to guide his cock to her entrance. He pushed the tip inside and paused.

She was wiggling around, panting, and still trying to pull him closer with her hands.

Luca took a deep breath before he plunged inside in one smooth thrust. Jade cried out as he filled her. Tightening his hold, he pulled back before he slammed inside. He repeated this over and over.

God, it felt so good to have her pussy clamp down on his cock. Each time he withdrew she clenched like she was trying to hold him in. He used his strength to powerfully thrust back.

Sweat dripped from the back of his neck. His hands grew damp where he held onto her. He was close to finding his climax but he needed to throw her over the edge first.

He picked up his pace even more. Using his shifter speed, he snapped his hips until Jade was practically screaming. When she did orgasm, she raked her nails down his shoulders and shuddered hard.

Luca was right there behind her. He pumped a few more times and his cum was filling her. Her legs shook as he strained to hold both of them up. He really should have taken her to bed but he hadn't been able to wait another minute.

As gently as he could, he helped Jade move her feet to the ground. He slipped out of her and rested his forehead on hers. She opened her eyes. The brightness of them was full of warmth.

His breath, which he was still struggling for, caught. She was so gorgeous. He didn't know how he'd got so lucky as to have her there with him, but he thanked his lucky stars that she was. He gripped her hand in his and pulled her along with him to the bedroom.

She followed behind without a word. Once they entered he guided her to the mattress. "Climb in," he said. "I'll grab us a bottle of water and lock up."

Jade yawned but nodded. She looked to be just moments away from sleep. He knew it wasn't just his lovemaking—it had been a very late night and they'd been busy. Jade rolled onto her stomach and buried her face into the pillow. Luca lifted the light sheet to cover her before he strolled from the room.

Chapter Seven

Jade slipped out of bed carefully to avoid waking Luca. It was just a little past eleven so they had almost two hours before they needed to be at Zak's place for the meeting. She turned back towards the bed and Luca's naked body on top of the covers. He'd been a passionate lover, and she had to resist the temptation to rejoin him in bed. She wanted to do a little more research on what was going on with the shifters.

She spotted a pair of sweatpants and a T-shirt on top of the nightstand. She pulled on Luca's clothes before exiting the bedroom and closing the door behind her.

Luca hadn't given her a tour earlier but the apartment was small so she'd spotted the kitchen when they'd made their way to his bedroom. Across from Luca's room was what she assumed Abilene had claimed, even if she never used it. The bed was made but that was the only furniture inside.

She stopped in the bathroom and washed her hands and face. She picked up the toothpaste and squeezed some onto her finger then brushed her teeth as best she could. That was one thing she needed to add to her go-bag—a toothbrush—especially if she was going to be hanging out with Luca more often. And she did hope for some more overnight visits with him.

Refreshed, she headed on to the kitchen. By the lack of clutter and pictures she suspected that Luca had not been staying there long. If he remained on the task force or transferred to the Coalition full-time she hoped that he would consider putting down some roots in Lake Worth. That would put them closer together and give them time to explore what was happening between them.

She strolled through the living room right into the kitchen. It wasn't big but would serve her purpose. The coffee pot was easy to find and she went about brewing a pot. While she waited, she retrieved her bag from next to the front door. She grinned, remembering what had happened earlier against that very door. Her body heated just thinking about it. Resolved to get her work done quickly so that she could go and wake Luca with some fun, she hurried back to the kitchen table.

Jade pulled her laptop from her bag and set it on top of the beautiful wood surface. She had to give Luca credit. He might not have a lot in his apartment but the furniture he did have was high quality. She pressed the power button before striding back to the coffee pot.

It wasn't hard to find the cabinet with the mugs or the canister of sugar. While it looked as though Luca didn't eat at home much, he had enough coffee, creamer and sugar. She'd found both vanilla and original creamer inside the fridge. Other than a few bottles of beer, that was it.

They'd have to spend some time at her house in the middle of the city. She loved to cook and could offer

Luca some comfort food. Last night when she'd been looking into the files of the shifters, she'd also run a Google search on coyote shifter traits. They were pack animals and needed the touch of family and home. Since Luca was away from his loved ones she'd see about making him feel comfortable with her.

It was natural for her to pay attention to what was going on around her. What better way to observe the shifters in her presence? She'd noticed that the wolves had stayed by each other's sides the entire night. Jamie and Zak were more solitary and with the exception of Abilene for Zak she could see them happy to work alone. She wondered how that affected their teams. Luca's information about the units of the Coalition was pretty helpful in understanding the men. She looked forward to seeing more.

The barbecue should help with that too. Other than setting up a plan for how to handle the investigation into the FBI, she would also get to see all the teams together. The night before they had been split so she hadn't been able to observe the birds, bears or felines. She really wanted the chance to. She was excited by the prospect of them all working together. That was the reason she'd wanted to be a part of the project in the first place — other than allowing her partner to be around others like himself.

Jade blew on her coffee while she walked back over to the table. Her laptop had loaded and was waiting. She typed in her password ready to start. She double clicked the folder she'd transferred the files into earlier.

There were three cases that concerned her. Luckily, Cole hadn't been involved in them, but she did recognise one name. Shannon Barber was listed as a fox shifter. She'd gone missing after investigating a missing person case about two years ago. The report stated that Shannon had disregarded orders and followed the suspects on foot alone. She hadn't been seen again.

As far as Jade could see, there hadn't been a real attempt to find the missing agent. That pissed her off. There was no telling if Shannon was out there captured and needing to be rescued. Instead of sending agents to find Shannon, the case had been closed. She searched the records and was disgusted to find that there hadn't even been a missing civilian on the case she had been on. The supervisor claimed that they had received bad information.

In a Word document she wrote up the highlights and a few questions she had about the case. Once that was completed she moved on to the next.

She lost herself in work, drinking her coffee, getting up once for a refill before she had her thoughts down in one place. Six different suspicious assignments resulting in the death or disappearance of the shifter agents. And that was only at her office. How many other divisions were going through the same? Even though she had access to her department files, she couldn't go further than that. She wanted to compare what she'd found with Sam Westby's own concerns. One thing for sure was that Luca was on to something.

She finished her second cup of coffee then glanced at the clock on the kitchen wall. Forty-five minutes had passed. That would give her a little time to wake Luca before she could talk with Sam.

She rose, leaving her mug and computer where they were to return to the bedroom. Luca's bedroom door opened quietly as she pushed on it. He was still in bed but had rolled over onto his back. She had enjoyed the view of his muscular shoulders and tight ass when she'd left him but this sight was even better.

His cock was already half-hard and waiting. She stripped off the borrowed clothes before she crawled up from the end of the bed. She slid her hands over his lower legs and Luca started to move.

"I wondered where you went," he said.

Grinning, she glanced up at him to find his eyes on her. "Did you miss me?" she asked.

"Oh yeah," he replied. "Why don't you come up here and I'll show you how much."

She had a better idea. She gently grasped his erection before running her hand up and down. His groan filled the quiet room while he bucked into her hold. She bent down to slowly tease the tip of his cock with her tongue.

"Jade," his voice was hoarse when he called her name.

She hummed then lowered farther onto him. His unique flavour was strong as she licked and sucked. Jade enjoyed the taste of him. Boldly she wrapped her hand around the base of him before picking up her tempo. Luca pushed up into her but not forcefully. He buried his hand in her hair, gripping tight.

Perfect, she loved this.

Bobbing her head, she brought him close to release before she backed away and popped off his cock. He growled in frustration, reaching for her. She let him pull her up to his chest.

"That was good," he complimented.

"Yeah?" she teased.

He lifted his head to kiss her softly. "This will be even better."

In an instant she found herself flipped onto her stomach with him plastered to her back. She tried to rise to her knees but he easily held her down. "I love your strength," she told him.

"I know." He ran his mouth over the back of her neck. "You tremble when you're under me. I could grow addicted to the way your body responds to me."

She could, too. He was also right about how she reacted to him. Even now she shuddered with need. "Please," she whined trying to move into him. She felt the tip of his cock at her entrance.

"This what you want?" he asked, still not entering but letting her feel how hard he was.

"Yessss," she hissed. If she didn't get him to make love to her again she was going to die.

"We didn't talk about condoms last night. I lost my mind and didn't even think to tell you we didn't need them if you didn't want to use them. I'm clean but I don't get sick either. My body recovers from any illness and I can't pass anything on to you. But that doesn't include birth control," he said.

He wanted to talk about this now? When she was going out of her mind for him? "I know. I know it all. And we're good on the birth control," she quickly assured him. "Just take me." Okay, maybe she shouldn't have let him know just how much she wanted him but she did. She wasn't one for playing games and she wasn't about to start now. If he wanted her to beg, she would.

He plunged inside, taking her with one strong solid thrust. Jade dropped her forehead onto the bed. He felt so good filling her up. Like he was built for her. He gripped her hips raising her lower body off the bed before he pulled out slowly. She didn't have time to complain before he slammed back inside.

Just like the night before he took her hard and fast. Still she pleaded for more. Repeated the request over and over.

"I'll give you all you need," he promised as he continued to ride her.

Jade could feel her climax building. Her toes tingled. Her vision began to grow white. One more hard thrust and she let go. She let her body override her brain. Vaguely she could hear Luca's roar as he joined her.

She dropped down onto the soft mattress when his hold loosened. He fell on top of her, both of them struggling to catch their breath. After what might have been an eternity or five minutes he slipped out of her and rolled onto his back. She turned her head to peer over at him. "That was awesome."

He laughed. "Intense. I didn't hurt you, did I?" He looked worried as he asked.

Jade had to smile at him. "Oh no, and I loved every minute of it."

"Good." He nodded. "I guess we have to get up to shower soon, though."

She closed her eyes. "Just give me a minute. I'm not sure my legs will hold me up."

Luca patted her ass. 'I'll grab your bag and start the shower. We can save time and take one together."

Even though her face was hidden in the bed she grinned. "Save time? Yeah right."

"I'm just trying to conserve water," he said.

She didn't believe him for a second. She felt the mattress move as he rose.

"Don't fall asleep."

"Hmm," she managed, already giving in to the desire for a nap.

* * * *

"It's your fault we're late," Luca told her as they pulled up in front of Zak's house. There were already several vehicles parked in the drive and on the street. They had to park across and in front of a neighbour's home.

"No way. You're the one who joined me in the shower," she argued.

"I wouldn't have had to if you hadn't taken a nap," he pointed out.

"You wore me out," she told him. "And you couldn't keep your hands to yourself when I was trying to wash up."

"You were naked and wet," he claimed. "No man could resist that."

Jade laughed while grabbing his hand as they reached Zak's sidewalk. Luca was fun to be with even out of bed. She'd not had a serious relationship in years. Not since she'd first joined the FBI. Her boyfriend at the time hadn't liked her hours or the fact that she worked on her research more than spending time with him.

Three months after making it to the agency she'd been alone. And she'd been okay with that. Her work kept her busy and she had good friends and a great partner. But now that she'd met Luca she found herself wishing she'd known him longer.

"They'll probably give us a hard time," Luca told her as they made it to the front door. "Don't let it bother you. Especially Zak. I gave him a hard time when he started up with Abilene."

"That's what friends do," she replied.

"Yeah," he agreed. "They can be annoying."

She knew it didn't really bother him. Before they knocked, the front door opened to show Jamie standing there with a huge shit-eating grin on his face.

"Did you bring the chips?" Jamie asked instead of greeting them. They both raised the grocery sacks. Luca had gone to his neighbourhood grocery to pick up what they needed while he'd let her sleep.

"Damn, I bet you would have forgotten," Jamie said as he allowed them in. "You know, since you were busy with other things."

"Of course not. I know how you get when you don't have your junk food," Luca replied with a smirk.

"Glad you could join us," Zak called out as they entered the hall.

"We're ten minutes late and I don't see Cody's truck," Luca yelled back.

"He's got you there." Jamie cackled. "I told you Cody would be the last one here."

She followed Luca into the living room and handed the bags to Mitch as he held his hands out. She glanced around the room and spotted Sam. She let go of Luca and strolled over. "Hey, Sam."

He seemed surprised but smiled back. "Hi."

Jade felt for him. Luca had explained everything that Sam had told him and she could see how much Sam's actions towards his ex-partner affected him. She wanted to offer him her friendship. "Where's Patrick?"

"He's back at the hotel. He doesn't think this is a good idea. I tried to talk to him — Cole did too — but he just doesn't want to get involved," Sam informed her.

She frowned. How could anyone be against helping their fellow agents? "I'm sorry to hear that."

Sam shrugged. "I don't know that this is a good idea either. It's not like anyone is going to listen to us."

"Someone already is," she told him. "With the Coalition and the ATF on our side we can help those who need it."

"And if it's already too late?" he asked.

Jade knew that in some of the shifter cases it *was* already too late. The ones that had been killed in the line of duty couldn't be brought back. But they could get justice. "We help who we can."

Sam shook his head. "That's what I joined the agency for. I wanted to help people. My dad, uncle and grandfather were all part of it before me. Now I wish I'd just become a cop. I wouldn't be mixed up in any of this."

Since she wasn't sure what to say she remained silent and let him vent.

"What kind of person am I? That I would turn my back on my partner? You think that makes me feel good? I know I'm an asshole!"

As his voice rose the others in the room started to pay attention.

"I don't think you're an asshole," she said. "I also don't think you don't care. You're here, right?"

He nodded. "I need some air."

She let him stalk off, unsure how to help.

Abilene walked up to her. "He's having a rough time. Your partner told me he thinks Patrick not coming is making Sam question the value of this meeting."

Jade nodded. "I can understand that," she admitted. "But we still have agents out there in danger. I can't believe I didn't pick up on the threat myself. To be honest I've been worried about Cole. But with my expertise I should have kept a better eye on the other shifters." She was so damn frustrated.

"You kept your partner safe. If he'd been moved into another division he might not be here now. Which means you wouldn't have wanted to join the task force. We'll figure this out," Abilene stated firmly.

"You're right. We can't change the past," Jade said.

"Now" — Abilene linked her arm with Jade's — "why don't we go check on the fire?"

"Okay," she agreed. She let Abilene lead her towards the door to get her alone, which is what she suspected Luca's partner really wanted.

Abilene pulled her from the room. Jade glanced over her shoulder and saw Cole cornering Luca. *Oh, this should be fun.* "Did you and Cole plan this?" she had to ask.

"I don't know what you're talking about. I just want to make sure you feel welcome and we need to get the meeting started," Abilene obviously lied.

Jade would just go with it, then. They strolled through the kitchen to the back door that led them to the deck. Zak was already in front of the pit.

Sam was across the yard staring out into space away from everyone. She spotted Ryder and Calvin filling ice chests with beer and soda.

"Want a beer?" Abilene offered.

"Sure." While Abilene walked over to the drinks, she took a seat at the patio table. It was long, made out of solid wood, with an umbrella to shelter from the sun. In Lake Worth it was important to have plenty of shade. It was hot even in the winter time. Cole had once mentioned that was a big reason that so many shifters had chosen the city as their home. The birds and other shifters that needed water had the lake. The ones that were used to hot weather were comfortable in the dry heat. The north of town led back into caves and caverns hidden in the mountains. Perfect to run in their animal form.

Abilene returned with two cold bottles and handed her one. "So…"

Jade popped the top of her brew. "Yes?"

"What are your intentions towards my partner?" Abilene asked as she sat across from her.

"You mean besides the hot sex?" she responded with a straight face.

Abilene scowled at her.

"I like Luca. He's smart and fun. I'm not sure where our relationship is going to go from here, but I would like to find out," she admitted. She couldn't blame Abilene for wanting to protect her partner. If it was Cole, she would do her own interrogation.

"That's good. Luca hasn't really dated seriously but I can tell he really likes you," Abilene told her. "But he is different. Have you ever dated a shifter before?"

"No, I haven't," she replied. "But I don't think of Luca as a shifter first. He's just a guy I'm interested in who happens to have that ability."

"Okay, I was worried you were using him. Cole said you wouldn't do that and got really pissed off when I suggested it but I had to make sure," Abilene said.

"Using him?" Jade didn't see where that would have come from.

"You're a shifter behaviorist. What better way to get your research than hooking up with a shifter? Luca happens to be one and finds you attractive," Abilene said.

Jade opened her mouth, but Abilene shook her head. "I realise it sounds stupid and insulting but I just don't want to see Luca hurt. I spoke to Cole and the other wolf shifters. I'll admit I didn't know if I could believe your partner but everyone else loves you."

She was insulted. Abilene had basically called her a slut who would sleep with Luca for her work.

"I told you not to say anything," Zak said as he joined them. He sat next to Abilene before draping an arm over her shoulder. "Abilene really doesn't mean any offence but thinks it's her job to watch over Luca since his family isn't here."

"Luca is a grown ass man. And not only does it question my integrity but also his. I think you should trust him to know what he wants," Jade spat.

"I agree," Luca said as he stepped up behind her.

Jade glanced over her shoulder. He was frowning at his partner. "Like I just told Cole, no one needs to worry about what's going on between Jade and me. I'll take the teasing but I won't stand for anyone grilling either of us. We're adults."

Jade smiled at him before offering her hand. He accepted her gesture, taking a seat beside her before lifting her fingers to his mouth and kissing them. Jade turned back to Abilene and Zak. She raised an eyebrow, daring either to comment. Zak smiled while Abilene nodded.

"Okay." Abilene lifted both hands. "I'm sorry. I won't say anything else. Good luck keeping Sal from butting in, though."

Luca was in the middle of stealing a drink of her beer. He slowly lowered the bottle from his lips. "Sal?"

"He couldn't get hold of you earlier so he called my cell. He asked me to tell you that he'll be here tomorrow morning with the information you requested."

"He's coming here?" Luca sounded weird.

Jade looked over at him. Luca had paled considerably. It was all she could do not to jump up and yell. Was he embarrassed by her? Why would he have a problem with his brother meeting her?

Just as she was about to excuse herself, Luca turned and grabbed her hand. "Marry me. Let's run away together, right now!"

"What?" she shrieked.

Zak and Abilene started to laugh loudly.

"I mean it," Luca pleaded. "After you meet Sal you won't want anything to do with me and my screwed-up brother. I like you and I don't want you to be scared away."

Completely confused, she looked from him to the others at the table. Zak was wiping tears from his eyes while Abilene grinned. She didn't understand what was happening. "What are you talking about? Are you nuts?" How had they gone from her thinking he was ashamed to a marriage proposal?

"Okay, it's a little soon to get married, I'll give you that. Let's just go away instead." Luca was squeezing her hands.

"Umm." She wasn't sure what to say.

The back door opened and the rest of the group started to trickle outside. They all looked at Zak and Abilene trying to get control of themselves, back to her and Luca.

"Cody's here," Jamie told them. "What'd I miss?"

"Luca just proposed to Jade so they could run away together and she wouldn't have to meet Sal," Zak told everyone.

"What?" Cole shouted. His question was drowned out by everyone else's mirth at what was happening.

"I've entered The Twilight Zone," Jade said.

"Nah," Jamie stated as he sat on her right. "Luca just doesn't want his big bro to scare you away."

Luca dropped his head onto the table and banged it a couple of of times. "I knew this was too good to be true."

Jade shared a confused look with her partner before placing her hand on the back of Luca's neck. "Are you okay?"

He turned his head to stare up at her. "We really should go on a long vacation."

Chapter Eight

Luca passed Jade another beer before he sat back down next to her. Once he'd explained how Sal loved to order him around and that he took his job as the elder brother too seriously, Jade stopped looking at him like he'd grown a second head or something. Okay, so he shouldn't have actually asked her to marry him but he'd panicked. He knew his brother, and Sal would give Jade the third degree. He just wanted to spare her. Well, that and he really wanted to get laid again. If Sal scared Jade off his chances weren't good. He hadn't been attracted to anyone before in the way he was to Jade.

Cole was still glaring at him but Jade had relaxed against his side. He'd taken a lot of ribbing during lunch but now that they'd settled around the living room and were discussing the case, everyone had seemingly remembered what they were there for.

He glanced over at Sam who was across from him sitting against the wall. Sam hadn't said much and that worried Luca. He was doing this for him, and now Sam was having second thoughts. Luca had overheard what Sam had said to Jade earlier, and he could understand Sam's fear, but Luca could not leave shifters in danger.

Jade had started the meeting by telling them about the reports she'd uncovered and the agents in her office who had been killed or were missing. She wanted to look into the three shifters who might still be alive. One female fox shifter, a leopard shifter and a deer shifter. Since their bodies hadn't been found and no one in the FBI was currently looking into their disappearances, Luca didn't see why they shouldn't try to find them.

"I'll talk to the commander first thing in the morning," Cody told them. "With all this information and what Sal is bringing us, we should be able to convince him that this is urgent."

"Do you really think he'll agree to look into this?" Sam spoke up for the first time.

"I do," Cody assured him. "This is what the Coalition was founded for. To protect shifters. Yes, we police our own kind to keep humans safe, but we also need someone looking out for shifters."

"I should have said something sooner," Sam said quietly.

"It's not your fault. There were enough problems to have tipped us off to look into it before. That's in the past and we can't change it. Now we just have to do whatever is in our power to help," Cody told him.

Sam sighed before nodding. Luca leant closer to Jade. "We need to look into his ex-partner. See if we can get him on our side."

"That's a good idea," she whispered. "Having inside information would really help."

"I'll try to get Sal to contact him. My brother has pull with the agency that not even the Coalition does," he said.

Jade grinned. "It seems like this brother might just come in handy."

"Sure, with the investigation," he groused. "But he treats me like I'm still sixteen. It drives me crazy. When he found out I got shot on my last assignment he flew down here to confront Zak."

"Really?" she laughed. "I would like to have seen that. Zak doesn't seem like the type to be intimidated by anyone."

"He isn't," Luca agreed. "It was quite funny how Zak riled Sal up." He'd been so embarrassed when Sal had yelled at Zak. Zak had shrugged it off and acted as though it didn't matter. When Sal had found out that Zak was interested in Abilene he'd cornered Zak and given him 'the talk'. Abilene was important to Luca so she was considered part of the family. She'd joined him several times when he'd gone home to visit and they loved her. At the time Luca had found it amusing but now that it was about to happen to him he wasn't so happy.

"I look forward to meeting him," Jade told him.

He groaned. She had no idea what she was in for.

"I think we'll break into smaller teams and work each case at the same time," Cody stated. "Right now we only have Cole and Jade's office files but hopefully we'll get others. So we'll all be picking up more than one here soon."

"How do you want us to split up?" Jamie asked.

Jamie specialised in missing persons and would be an asset. Luca would love to work with Jamie on this.

"You have the experience. Why don't you take the FBI and ATF for your team," Cody suggested. "Zak's team and the wolves will take one, and mine will take the third."

Everyone in the room nodded in agreement. Luca would get a chance to work beside Jamie and also Jade. That couldn't have worked out any better.

"Jade, why don't you email what you have to everyone and we can get started. We'll work here for a couple of of hours so we have even more intel to give the commander. If anyone has any resources they can call, use them. Right now it might be unofficial but I don't think too many people will question us," Cody ordered.

"We'll spread out in the kitchen," Zak said standing. "Cody, why doesn't your group take the dining room and Jamie's can remain here?"

Jade was already busy typing on her laptop, probably emailing her file to the others, so Luca stood. "I'll get us some more drinks," he offered.

As the three different units separated, Luca really had to give them credit. These agents were using their free day to start an investigation on their own in order to help others. He was glad he'd brought up his concerns.

He pushed open the kitchen door and saw that Brady and Mitch already had their computers starting up. Zak stood at the counter, filling the coffee pot. "I'll bring some out when it's brewed," Zak told him.

"I'll just grab some bottles of water for now," Luca said. He did that, but when he turned to go back to the living room Zak had stepped in front of him.

"You doing okay?" he asked quietly.

"Yeah, sure," Luca replied, surprised. He was fine and he wasn't sure why Zak was asking.

"It's a lot to deal with. You're not even fully healed from the last assignment and now we're taking this on. I don't know how the others feel, but I think this is going to be a battle. The FBI isn't just going to roll over and let us look into their agents. Even with the commander's say. It could get dangerous," Zak said.

"You're probably right but I have to see this through," Luca replied.

"Just make sure you're careful." Zak pointed at him.

"I already have one big brother on the way so I don't need another," Luca teased. He was touched that Zak cared about him but he knew how to handle himself.

"I'm going to let you comparing me to your brother go," Zak said with a scowl.

Luca just smiled before he walked past him to join his team. Zak lightly slapped the back of his head, shocking Luca.

He passed Cody's unit in the dining room. The area didn't get a lot of use as far as Luca knew, but there was plenty of room for the birds of prey division.

Jamie had moved to one of the recliners and had some papers spread out in front of him. Luca passed him a bottle of water before rejoining Jade on the couch. She had kicked her shoes off and was sitting cross-legged with her laptop.

She was gorgeous, giving all her attention to whatever she was doing.

"What can I help with?" he asked.

Jamie passed him over one of the pages. "See if you can find any names in there that we might be able to contact. Preferably shifters. They'll probably be more than willing to talk to us. Especially if they know something is going on."

"Got it," Luca said. He read through the report looking for names of any of the other agents who had been with Shannon Barber before she'd gone missing. He pulled out his notepad and started to work on who might be able to assist them. He'd first need to find out whether or not they were shifters. He hoped to find something important.

* * * *

Luca pulled his SUV in front of Jade's house and peered at the small brick home. The green grass looked full and rich. The porch light was on, illuminating the white wicker furniture she had placed under the large pane of glass. The curtains were currently closed but if he lived there he would keep them open to view the glorious area.

"This is it," Jade said before yanking the door handle to climb out.

He'd agreed to go home with her when they'd been leaving his place so he'd packed a bag with a few days' worth of clothing and his toiletries. Now that he was there, though, he was a little nervous. She'd seen his pathetic little apartment and now he was faced with her home. From the look of the outside he could only imagine how nice the inside would be.

"Are you coming?" She peered in from the open passenger door.

"Of course," he said and smiled. The more time he spent with her he was really starting to question what she saw in him. He was from a small town that was mainly occupied by relatives. He worked for the ATF because he enjoyed blowing shit up. He hadn't had many friends before he'd met the Coalition guys and he was feeling just a little lacking. Jade was brilliant. Back at Zak's house she'd easily connected two names to all the cases. She'd only read through the files Zak and Cody had but had remembered the names of the agents involved in the assignments.

Her catch had saved them all time and given them a direction to start looking in. Sam had even known one of the men and had told them how he would have seen him with his ex-partner. That concerned all of them. As glad as he was for the break in the case, Luca was feeling just a little bit self-conscience. Jade was obviously brilliant and he didn't know how long he'd be able to hold her interest. He wanted her with every part of him, his mind, body and soul. Hell, even the coyote inside seemed to calm when he was in her presence. Luca knew that was a sign of deep trust. There was just something about Jade that he recognised had potential for turning into a serious relationship. If he didn't mind putting his heart of the line. And he wasn't certain if he'd be able to. He'd never been in love before.

"Luca?"

Realizing that he had to make a decision, he pushed open his door then grabbed his bag from the back. After he slammed the door closed he strolled around the front of the vehicle to join her. She stood on the sidewalk waiting for him.

"You okay?" she asked with evident concern.

"Sure," he said. "I guess I'm just a little nervous.

She jolted. "What about?"

Why had he said that? He wanted to groan. But he might as well tell her everything. The worst that could happen was that she'd send him home. Maybe that would be for the best. It would only be more painful if she realised later that he was boring. "Well, for one thing… This." He waved his hand at her home.

"My house?"

"Yeah, it's beautiful. I have nothing to compare to it. My apartment here is empty but my condo isn't that much better and I don't have any excuse for that. I've lived there for five years!" he exclaimed.

"You just haven't found a place to put down roots. That doesn't mean you're lacking in any way. Hell, it might be perfect. If things work out between us you can move in with me. I love my house," she told him.

"Move in?" he teased. "I just might take you up on that."

She giggled before growing serious again. "That's not all that's bothering you, though."

"No," he admitted. "Want to sit?" He motioned to the porch chairs he'd admired minutes before.

"Sure." She turned and strolled up the steps. She set her bag by the front door before pulling out one of the chairs to sit on.

He set his bag beside his seat and settled across from her.

"What is it? I thought we were getting along pretty well. Is it the thing with your brother?" she asked softly.

"No—Well, I'm not happy about you meeting him. Like I said, he forgets that I'm a grown man and I don't want you to see me the way he does. I know I can be immature but I do make my own decisions," he answered.

"I have fun with you, Luca," she assured him. He believed she did but he just didn't think that it would last.

"I don't want you to get bored with me," he confessed.

"Bored?" she gasped. "Are you kidding me? I watched the training video of you and the Coalition the night before we met you. As soon as I heard your voice and listened to how much fun you were having I couldn't wait to meet you."

"That won't last. You'll eventually get tired of my antics. Everyone but Abilene does."

She was up on her feet in an instant. Before he knew what was happening she came around the table and planted herself in his lap. He grunted as she dropped down. Not because of her weight, but because he hadn't been expecting it.

"You're crazy," she told him.

"And you're very intelligent. Not only are you working for the FBI but you have your own research department in shifter behaviour. What you know is probably ten times more than me, and I'm a shifter."

"Luca." She cupped his face. "I like everything about you. All my life has been dedicated to gathering as much knowledge as possible. I've never been good at just letting go and enjoying myself. It's one of the reasons that while I'm a field agent I also specialise in another department."

"Okay." He wasn't sure what she was getting at but she was looking at him like she expected a response.

"So I need you to make me have fun. I want your power and passion in the bedroom and your sharp mind and quick wit outside of it," she explained.

That actually made him feel pretty good. "Yeah?"

"Yes," she agreed. "So why don't we go inside and you can get that incredible body of yours to nail me to the closest flat surface."

He was hard in an instant. Even as much as he was shocked by her words, his body was ready to follow the order. He tightened his arm around her waist to pull her closer. "How about a small sample?" he asked. He didn't give her time to reply. Instead he latched his mouth to hers.

She opened for him, allowing him to thrust his tongue inside. She moaned and he swallowed the sound.

"I love kissing you," he said when they parted.

"Well, by all means. Who am I to deny you the pleasure?" she murmured before moving back towards him.

"If we don't go inside right now I'm going to fuck you out here in full view of all your neighbours," he told her seriously.

She grinned. "Really?"

"Let's not find out," he replied. He stood, picking her up easily, and stalked to the front door. "Keys?"

"Front pocket of my bag."

Damn, he had to put her down in order to reach her bag. He set her on her feet before bending to pick it up. He searched through the pocket until he found the small key chain. He quickly unlocked the door before turning back to her. He held out his hand. She grasped the handle of his bag before moving to him. He took his pack from her hands then set it down beside hers right inside the door. Yanking her closer, he fastened his lips over hers.

As they kissed he moved her farther into the cool interior of the house. Another reason to keep their lovemaking out of public. Blessed air conditioning. He slammed the front door closed, but instead of backing her into it he gently pulled her to the floor.

Luckily, her entryway was carpeted so when their knees hit the ground there was cushion. He started to undress her slowly. When he had to remove his mouth from hers to pull her T-shirt over her head she gasped.

"You're so hot," he told her.

"You too," she said. "I need you naked now." She pushed his hands away and started to unsnap her pants herself. Luca matched her article for article until they were both bared.

He ran his gaze over her body as she laid back. Her tanned skin was already glistening with a fine layer of sweat. He bent and captured her pert nipple between his lips. She arched her back, pressing into him.

"Touch me," she pleaded.

No problem there. While he sucked her, drawing out soft cries, he ran his palm down her stomach to her wet folds. He brushed over her a couple of of times before sliding his fingers from her folds. With two digits he entered her pussy.

She moaned long and low.

He pumped his fingers in and out several times.

"Please, Luca, now."

Luca lifted his head to peer down at her.

"I want you," she murmured.

He slid his hands to her hips and lifted her. Scooting closer, he positioned himself at her entrance. He slowly pushed in between her folds and penetrated her. He drew out just as slowly so that she felt every inch of him. He was proud of his full eight inches. He wanted to take his time. The previous times he'd made love to her they'd had passion and heat. Now he wanted to show her how much he cared.

"More," she demanded.

Luca only shook his head. He thrust just as gently until she was fully wrapped around his cock. Her inner muscles clenched around his hard member. He groaned in pleasure.

It was wonderful. This feeling of complete connection between the two of them. She lifted her head and glared at him.

"Luca!"

He grinned and withdrew at the same pace. She growled as she pushed her hands under her and lifted. She repositioned herself on his lap. "Now I'm in charge," she told him.

It wasn't what he'd had planned but he could work with this. "Go ahead."

Gripping his shoulders tightly, she rose up, causing his cock to slide out before she dropped back down. He held onto her waist but allowed her to set the pace. She rode him hard, head back and eyes closed, until he had no choice but to buck up and meet her body each time she slammed back down.

They rocked, panting and gasping, until she screamed, crying out her climax. Luca held her close, finally thrusting until he reached his own release.

She blew her hair out of her face. "It just gets better and better."

He chuckled. "I'm really considering asking you to marry me again."

"Oh God!" she groaned. "Don't start with that again."

"You should have seen your face," he told her. "It was classic." It really had been.

"I would punch you but I'm too tired," she claimed.

"How about a shower and then bed? We're going to have a long day tomorrow with the added benefit that you get to meet my brother."

"Oh yippy," she joked then she yawned.

"Up you go." He pushed her off his lap.

She grumbled but eventually climbed to her feet. She held her hand out to him. He accepted the offer and soon they were both standing in her front entryway naked. "Tour?" he asked.

"The kitchen is back through there." She waved behind them. "Living room and a restroom down here." She tugged him along. "I'll take you to my room. The other rooms up here" — she started up the stairs — "are my office and the guest bedroom. Explore all you want. Just after I fall flat on my face in my nice comfortable bed."

"You got it," he told her. He tried to take in everything as she pulled him along. Her carpet was a light tanned and went well with the cream coloured walls. The house wasn't big but she had plenty of room. He liked the homey feel to the place.

Her bedroom door stood open and they entered. The bed was unmade and did in fact look very soft. The comforter was black but the light sheets matched the colour of her walls.

There were several pictures on the wall, all done in black and white. There was the Eiffel Tower, Brooklyn Bridge, Golden Gate Bridge and some other places he wasn't close enough to see yet.

"I have an attached bathroom here so we can shower together," she told him.

"We'd better get to it before you fall asleep in there," he teased her.

"Just keep your hands to yourself," she ordered.

"I promise," he said, not meaning it at all.

* * * *

Luca's phone buzzed from the nightstand next to his head. He rolled over and picked it up before the sound woke Jade. "It's five in the morning," he griped as a greeting.

"Where the hell are you?" Sal demanded.

"In bed, asleep, like normal people," he whispered back to his brother.

"Since I'm currently standing in your bedroom I know that's a lie," Sal sniped.

"I didn't say I was in *my* bed," he pointed out. "And why are you in my apartment?"

"Didn't Abilene tell you I was coming?" Sal questioned. There was movement on the other end of the phone, and Luca didn't want to think about what his brother would be going through of his.

"She did," he said. "But I didn't expect you in my place before dawn."

"We caught an early flight. Now answer my question," Sal ordered.

"I'm obviously at someone else's place. Just take a nap or something and meet me at the office in a couple of of hours," he replied. "I might even bring you in donuts if you're a good boy."

Sal growled. "Don't push it."

Luca laughed. "See you later." He hung up before Sal could say anything further. Oh sure, he would pay for it later, but he enjoyed screwing with his eldest sibling.

"Your brother got in?" Jade asked from the other side of the bed.

Luca set his cell back down before he rolled over and faced her. She had her chin resting on her fist while she watched him.

"Good morning," he greeted before kissing her lightly.

"Hmm, let's try that again," she said as she reached for him.

Luca climbed on top of her. "Okay."

Chapter Nine

True to his word, Luca picked up six dozen donuts on the way to the office. Jade teased him but Luca knew that Sal wouldn't have appreciated his smart mouth earlier and he needed to make it up to his brother. It wasn't Sal's fault that he was such a hard ass. He'd always had the job of taking care of the other Perez kids. That was just the way it was in his family. As first born it had fallen to him to set a good example for the younger kids.

As the baby, Luca had got away with more than anyone else. He'd partied hard and stayed out late in high school. It was always Sal who would pull him out of all the trouble he found himself in. He never ratted Luca out to his parents but Sal could sure lecture for hours.

Yet, even though Sal could be overbearing and demanding, he was a great big brother. Luca just had a hard time convincing Sal that he was grown up now and could make his own decisions.

Jade pushed open the conference room door and all conversation stopped. He followed her in, holding up the boxes. The scent from the freshly baked goods was mouthwatering. "I brought breakfast," he announced.

"Awesome!" Jamie cried. "And you didn't even let having sex make you late."

Jade made a choking sound as Jamie howled with laughter. Luca glanced over at his friend, noticing that he had his hand on the back of Sal's chair. Jamie had set that up nicely.

"Sorry, Jamie," Luca said with a smirk. "I know Brandy is making you watch your diet and I wouldn't want to do anything to upset her. I think you should refrain."

Jamie grumbled while he stalked closer to Luca. "What she doesn't know won't hurt me," he stated as he grabbed the load from Luca.

"Well, I don't know…" Luca replied. "It might come up the next time we talk."

Jamie flipped him off. Luca chuckled until he saw Sal's glare. "What?" he snapped. Shit, he sounded like a teenager again.

Sal slowly shook his head before rising from his chair. He looked at Luca before settling his gaze on Jade. Luca wanted to jump in front of her to keep her from his brother. He knew it wouldn't work, though. When Sal was determined, nothing that Luca said or did mattered.

"So, you're the woman my baby bro is shacking up with," Sal said to Jade.

"Sal!" Luca shouted. God, he wanted to throttle his brother already.

"Sal!" Flynn, Sal's partner, yelled.

"Hey, asshole!" Cole jumped to his feet.

Jade laughed. "No."

Sal ignored everyone but Jade. "No?"

"We're not shacking up. Just using each other's body in every imaginable way possible," she said with a straight face.

There was no movement, no talking—he wasn't even sure if anyone was breathing—as they all waited for Sal's reaction.

Luca waited until Sal nodded. "Sounds good then," Sal told her. "Did you get any lemon filled?"

Luca just stared at his brother as Sal started opening lids. *What the fuck?* He glanced over at Jade but she only shrugged before walking over to her partner. Cole put his arm over her shoulder as he continued to glare at Sal. Jade whispered something to him, which drew his attention away from his brother. Luca really didn't want to get in-between Cole and his brother if Cole decided not to let Sal's comment go. He knew it was his responsibility but why couldn't everyone just back off and give him and Jade time to figure out their relationship on their own? He stepped forward, hoping he could take Cole's attention from Sal. His brother's partner was normally really good at keeping Sal under control. Luca didn't know how Flynn managed it. If he had to work with Sal he'd strangle him in one day. And he loved Sal. Even now Flynn had his hand on Sal's shoulder, remaining by his side while Jade still spoke softly to Cole.

Cole cracked a smile before he reached for one of the boxes. The tension in the room seemed to evaporate as Cole relaxed. Luca hoped the crisis had passed for now. He joined the rest of the team and grabbed his own food. He noticed that Cody and Zak were missing. "Any word from the commander?" he asked. He sat next to his brother because he knew that Sal would just make a big deal out of it if he didn't.

"They're still in a meeting," Ryder informed him from across the table.

"I brought you some files I think you'll need. I already gave Cody a copy. He met up with me early," Sal said, sparing a quick scowl to Luca.

"That's why he's the boss," Luca retorted.

Sal sighed. Luca took a big bite from his donut as everyone else in the room settled down. Cole and Jade had their heads close together discussing something. Luca wondered what it was, especially when she grabbed her backpack and pulled out her laptop. She pushed her plate away and started working furiously.

"What's going on?" Luca asked his brother, knowing that Sal had a pretty good idea.

"I gave Cole several names I think they should look into," Sal told him.

The familiar tone that Sal used when talking about Jade's partner surprised him. "Do you know Cole?"

"Yes, we attended the academy together, although he was a few classes behind me. He's a good agent. Or he was before all this happened. I get the impression that he isn't too happy with the organisation now. Which is a real shame. Cole is an asset," Sal said.

"Why's he still there?" Luca questioned. It was something he was trying to understand about a lot of the shifters in the FBI. They hadn't been accepted and now it seemed that they were even being mistreated. Why had they stayed? Or come back after being suspended when the FBI had first learned that they were shifters?

"Cole's stubborn. He feels he has a right to work there and he is correct. He won't leave because he wants the others to see him standing up for his rights every day," Sal answered.

"That's why you're still there, isn't it?" Luca asked.

"Mainly," Sal admitted. "I'm lucky that I have a boss who respects my work. I'm a lot better off than most of the others and I've worked damn hard to get where I am today."

"Still, it would be easier if they just switched agencies," Luca commented.

"Perhaps, but someone needs to take a stand. That's what we're going to do here," Sal informed him. "Let the government know that we are equals in every way."

"You told your boss about the investigation?" Luca guessed.

"I have someone I answer to. I can't go off half-cocked at a whim. I needed his support and I have it," Sal confirmed.

"That's good. At least someone high up in the chain knows," Luca said.

"He's more than aware. The reason I was able to get the reports I wanted so quickly is because he was already looking into some claims," Sal told him.

"Really?" Luca asked, surprised. If the FBI was aware that there was a problem, why were shifters still being targeted?

"It's just suspicion right now, but he's doing what he can," Sal said.

The conference room door opened, and Cody and Zak joined them.

"The good news is Commander Green approved our request to start an investigation," Cody said as he took one of the remaining seats.

Zak remained standing and leant against the wall behind him.

"The bad news?" Jamie asked.

"He doesn't know how much he can help," Cody informed them. "The FBI have been pulling out all the stops to hinder anything we do with them. Even for local joint cases."

"They did agree to the joint task force so that's something," Jade commented.

Patrick cleared his throat. Luca and the others turned their attention to him. "About that..."

Sam grunted, appearing very unhappy. When Patrick didn't say anything for a minute Sam growled. "You tell them or I will," Sam threatened.

Patrick sat up straight in his chair and looked at Cody. "I was sent here to make sure the task force fails," he said quietly.

"What?" Luca yelled.

Cole's and Jade's jaws dropped while some of the others frowned. Jamie jumped to his feet, towering over Patrick.

Patrick held his hands up to ward off the questions being fired at him. "Let me explain," he said. "I was ordered by our boss to sabotage any training exercises and keep an eye on the other FBI agents. I have to report back every night on what we're doing."

"You told them about our suspicions?" Zak accused. His big arms were crossed over his chest while he glared at Patrick.

"Yesterday when you all met at Zak's house," Patrick confirmed.

Luca looked form Patrick, to Zak, to Cody. "You already knew that," he speculated.

"Yes," Zak answered. "Commander Green brought it up. He had a call from the agent in charge here in Lake Worth."

"Simmons?" Jade asked. "He's our boss, not Sam and Patrick's."

"Yes," Cody confirmed. "Simmons dropped enough clues to make Commander Green presume one of his agents was talking."

"He blamed me?" Jade guessed.

"He did," Cody replied.

"Commander Green questioned us this morning, but we assured him that you weren't the leak. Cole also wouldn't talk since it's shifters like him being targeted. That left the other two humans here. Having Simmons call instead of their boss was supposed to have us following the wrong line. Kick you and Cole out and hurt the investigation. You're the one who found the connections in all the cases," Zak explained.

"Son of a—" Jade yelled. She spun to Patrick, looking like she was going to lunge at him. Cole swiftly wrapped his arm around her neck and held her back.

"I'm sorry!" Patrick cried. "They told me if I didn't do it they'd reassign me to one of the shifter units! I don't want to die."

Cole was speaking into Jade's ear, which seemed to be calming her down. She relaxed into him but didn't stop shooting daggers at Patrick.

"When did you find out?" Luca asked Sam.

"This morning," Sam said. "I told Patrick that I was going to do this with or without him. He tried to talk me out of it and finally came clean about why we were really sent here."

"That's why you were so worried last night. Patrick said something to make you doubt yourself?" Luca questioned.

Sam nodded. "He asked me if it was worth my career and maybe my life."

What a fucking mess. Luca didn't even know where they should go from here. They had a rat in their ranks but at least they knew about him. Even if Patrick confessed to them, though, he could still screw up their assignment, if he hadn't already.

"This has made our jobs harder, but we still have work to do," Cole stated.

"I agree," Sal said. "Let me show you what I have."

"What about him?" Jade spat pointing at Patrick.

"Don't worry," Jamie replied with a grin. He put his arm over the back of Patrick's chair. "Patrick will be by my side the whole time."

Patrick swallowed visibly. Luca didn't blame him at all. Jamie was a great guy and fun to be around, but when he was in full agent mode he was scary as hell. Patrick would not be going against them again.

Sal accepted some printed papers from his partner and stood. While he walked to the front of the table, Sal's partner, Flynn O'Bannon, passed around more papers.

"I was able to find four other agents that have been killed or seriously injured in the line of duty since they announced what they were. I'd like to add these to the ones you've already discovered," Sal told them.

Luca read through the names and times that his brother had put together.

"Do you have access to the actual files?" Jade asked.

"Yes," Sal answered.

"I'd like to have a look to compare the names to the ones I'm already researching," she told him.

Sal nodded to Flynn who started to pull out his computer. Jade lifted her bag and followed suit. He pulled his attention back to his brother as Sal started to tell them about each case and what had happened to the shifter who had been on assignment.

"I notice that in all these reports there was only one shifter involved," Cole said. "The rest of the agents were humans."

"I picked up on that too," Flynn spoke up. "I looked through their records to see when they were transferred as part of that team. It's anywhere between one and six months."

"That's..." Cole and Jade exchanged looks. Luca knew what they were thinking. If the other shifters had been assigned human partners and given a big assignment there was a chance that Cole would have also been hurt or worse.

"We think there's a plan to take you out. Sending you here? Might be a part of it," Sal stated.

Jade paled and grasped Cole's arm. "They want to kill you!"

"Or at least make me disappear."

She was on her feet and had hold of Patrick. She jerked him up and shook him. "What's the plan?" she demanded.

"I don't know!" Patrick cried. "I swear. I was just supposed to keep them informed about what we're working on. Let them know about the training exercises."

Cole grabbed hold of Jade, making her release Patrick. She resisted for an instant. Luca hated to admit it but he was turned on by the display. Jade might be one of the few humans in the room but she was just as terrifying as any of them when riled up.

She was a force, and Luca wished that he could pull her away and show her how sexy he found her.

"So, if something happened to him here it wouldn't come back on them? Cole is pretty high profile in his department. He's been standing up for all the other shifters," Jade said while still glaring at Patrick. "They're being more careful this time."

"Patrick's already told them what we suspect, though," Jamie pointed out. "They can't really go after him now."

"They can if they move on it," Zak argued. "If they work quickly before we get our investigation started they have a chance. They don't know what Jade found or that Sal and Flynn are here. If Cole is hurt or killed, the suspicion falls on us. This might work out in our favour."

"So what do we do?" Jade asked, looking worried.

"We give them the ammo to shoot themselves," Zak said.

"What?" Jade turned towards Zak. "You are not going to use my partner as bait."

"It's okay." Cole patted her back.

"No!" she yelled. "Find another way."

"Normally I would agree with you." Sal walked over to her. "But Cole is a trained agent. He'll be okay."

"So were the others!" Jade argued.

"But they didn't know what was going to happen," Zak said. "Even if they suspected something wasn't right, I doubt they thought their own agency was trying to take them out."

"I don't like it," Jade said.

"We're all here for Cole. We know something could happen," Luca told her.

She frowned at him. "You agree with them?"

Luca wished that they were alone so he could take her in his arms. *Oh, screw it.* He rose to his feet and strolled over to her. She was staring at him with a look of shocked betrayal. "We have one more thing they don't know about."

"What's that?" she asked. He was glad that she didn't pull away from him.

"Patrick," he told her.

"What I am supposed to do?" Patrick asked.

"What you have been. You're going to keep your boss informed about what we're doing. We'll just be telling you what to say," Luca said.

"I can't... I can't do that. I don't want to get involved," Patrick whined.

Jade growled and lunged at him. Luca kept himself between the two of them, though.

"I don't think you have a choice, little man," Jamie told Patrick.

Jade grinned. "We can make you," she threatened.

"Fine." Patrick sank down further in his chair. "I'll do whatever you tell me."

"Good." Zak rubbed his hands together. "Looks like we have a training exercise to plan."

"What about the other agents?" Jade questioned.

"Send me everything you have," Sal said. "We'll find them."

Jade grabbed his hand and gave him a good squeeze. "We've got a lot of work to do."

* * * *

They broke for lunch so Luca pulled Jade out of the room and down the hall to another empty space. He closed the door behind them before pulling her into his arms.

She rested her head on his chest, just leaning into him and sighing deeply.

"We won't let anything happen to Cole," he promised.

"I can't help but worry. He's already been through so much, and to find out that someone wants to hurt him pisses me off. But that's not all of it. I believed in the FBI. Even after all the shit that went down with the shifters, I still knew that what I did was helping and I could make a difference," she said.

"And you are," he assured her.

"Really?" she scoffed. "I can't even keep my own agents safe. Now my partner's life is on the line. I'm so damn pissed off."

"I know, but you need to remember that it's just a few bigoted people and not everyone in the agency is involved in this."

"How are we going to be sure we catch everyone? We have enough to go on after my boss and Sam's office, but what about all the other people who've had a hand in this? The agents that betrayed their colleagues?"

"We do our job," Luca told her. "And trust that Sal will be able to bring down everyone involved. My brother may be a pain in the ass but he is good at his job."

"Okay," she said. She wrapped her arms around his waist. "I'm glad you're here. I like the other guys, but I feel better with you."

"You trust me, huh?" he teased.

She tilted her head back. "You could say that."

"So now that you've met my brother, what are your thoughts about us running away together and getting married?" he joked.

Jade laughed just like he wanted her to. "I don't know. I'm kind of high maintenance and always wanted a big wedding."

Since he wasn't sure whether she was joking or not, he nodded. "I guess we could do that. My mom would probably take over the planning, though. She's crazy at events, but I'm sure the two of you will get along."

Jade smacked him. "You're going to propose one of these days and I'm going to say yes just to make you go through with it."

The scary part of her statement was that Luca wasn't actually sure he would mind. Of course he'd only known her for two days, but he wasn't about to let her go. If Abilene could move in with Zak then Luca had high hopes for the two of them.

He placed his hand under her chin to tilt her face up. Lowering his mouth slowly, he watched her. Her lashes fluttered before she closed her eyes. Their lips met and Luca kept the kiss gentle. As much as he would love to ravish her, they were in the middle of the Coalition and that just couldn't happen.

Luca pulled back and smiled at her. "Calmer?" he asked.

She nodded. "Thanks."

"Oh, it was my pleasure," he told her. He kissed her once more gently before pulling away. "We'd better get back."

"I know," she said before slipping out of his embrace. She reached for the door and yanked it open.

Flynn was across the hall leaning up against the wall.

"What's going on?" he asked Flynn.

"Your brother wants to talk to you," Flynn informed him.

Luca peered down both sides of the hall. "Where is he?"

Flynn grinned. "He didn't want to hear the two of you start screwing around so he went to get some drinks from the vending machine."

Luca chuckled. "But you don't mind?" he teased. He liked Flynn and thought of him as another brother. Sal and Flynn had been partners for longer than he and Abilene, and Flynn was around the family just as much. He was calm and easy-going compared to Sal's overbearing ass.

"It's been a slow couple of of months for me," Flynn replied. "I don't mind."

Jade groaned. "I'll leave you boys to compare notes," she said.

Jade strolled back towards the conference room they'd been using. Loud footsteps behind him had Luca turning to see Sal walking towards him with two bottles of water.

"Done already?" Sal asked as he tossed Flynn one of the drinks.

"Very funny. I'm not messing around inside the Coalition," Luca told him.

"I would hope not, but you never know," Sal responded.

"I'll let you two catch up and check to see if the food is here yet," Flynn offered.

"Thanks, man." Sal tipped his head to his partner.

Luca leant his shoulder against the wall. "What's up?"

"I wanted to make sure you're okay," Sal replied.

"I'm good," Luca said.

"I saw your training exercise. You did a good job taking on the Coalition," Sal offered.

"Thanks, I'm having fun and learning a lot."

"You still thinking of transferring?" Sal asked.

He shrugged. "Probably. If this task force doesn't work out. I don't see Abilene going back either so at least I can keep her as my partner."

"Doesn't hurt that you're interested in a woman here."

Luca had wondered when Sal would get around to that. "You could say that. Why? You going to investigate her?"

"What makes you think I haven't already?"

Luca jerked his head up. "You're kidding."

Sal shrugged. "I had some time before you arrived this morning."

"What did you find?" Luca asked. He wasn't worried, though. Sal would have done it sooner or later. He would have warned her but she probably already knew.

"She is an excellent agent. She's received several awards and most of her superiors have only had good things to say about her in her evaluations."

"Okay," Luca urged him to continue.

"She is also very interested in the behaviour of shifters," Sal said.

"That's her job," he pointed out.

"And that doesn't bother you? That she could be using you to further her research?" Sal asked.

Luca laughed. "She didn't have to sleep with me in order to study me. I would have done it anyway. All of us would. Her research will help the academy training and hopefully help the relationship between humans and shifters get back on the right track. Any of us would have been happy to help."

"I had to ask," Sal told him. "You may be a grown man but you're still my little brother."

"I know," Luca said. "But please just try to remember that I'm a grown man like you said. I like Jade and I don't need you looking into her or threatening her."

"I won't," Sal promised. "I don't want to have to deal with Cole."

Luca laughed. He didn't blame his brother. "Anything else?"

"I really just wanted to check on you. You're still recovering."

"There's a little tenderness sometimes, but for the most part it doesn't bother me," Luca assured him.

"God, I still want to kill Zak when I think about it," Sal growled.

"I thought you two were getting along."

"We are," Sal said. "I just never got my chance at him."

"It'll be okay." Luca patted his brother's shoulder.

"Don't be a smart ass. I can still knock you into next week," Sal warned.

"Yes, sir." Luca held his hands out in front of him.

"And call Mom!" he ordered. "She worries."

"I promise." Luca threw his arm around his brother's shoulder. "So what happened with that girl you were seeing? Amanda?"

"Angela," Sal corrected as they walked down the hall.

"Well?" Luca pressed. Sal hated to talk about his personal business, although he had no problem sticking his nose into Luca's business.

Sal shrugged. "It didn't work out."

"Why not?" Luca asked. "Isn't that the fourth girl in four months? Damn, bro, you go through them fast."

"Shut up," Sal grumbled. "It just didn't work out."

Normally Luca would have given Sal a hard time, but Sal had gone easy on him so he didn't push his brother. Plus, he felt bad for him. Sal was actually looking for a woman to settle down with and couldn't seem to find the right woman who was in the same place in her life as him.

His brother deserved a good girl. Maybe after this was all over he would see who he could introduce Sal to. Or put his mom in charge. That would get her off his case while he explored his relationship with Jade.

Chapter Ten

Jade tested the temperature of the water before she climbed into the shower. They had a couple of of hours before the night's exercise and bait attempt, and she needed to unwind and work some tension from her shoulders. She hated the plan that they had come up with, or at least her role. There had been several heated discussions during the afternoon before a strategy had been agreed upon.

"Room for me?"

She turned her head and smiled at Luca. He had come back to her house so that they could freshen up and get ready. Jamie had taken Patrick and Sam back to his house while Sal and Flynn had gone with Cole. Jade was glad for the break but while she wanted to calm down she was too nervous. Maybe it was a good thing that Luca had joined her.

"Come here," she said, beckoning him closer.

Luca stepped inside the stall and pressed against her. Jade ran her gaze over his body. She loved the golden tint of his skin. It really made his dark hair and eyes stand out. He was already erect and her mouth watered for wanting to taste him.

She ran her hands over his muscular chest, enjoying the feel of him. Luca gripped her hips lightly, letting her take the lead. Jade leant forward and kissed his pecs before running her tongue down and over his nipple. He groaned, telling her that he liked it.

As she moved her lips to the other side, she grasped his cock with her right hand, pumping him. Luca pushed into her hold, the water spraying them easing their movements. "I need you to relax me," she told him.

"You have to promise not to fall asleep after, though," Luca teased. She deserved it since the other times they'd been together he'd worn her out.

"I'd take it as a compliment," she said.

"Oh, I do," he agreed. "But we only have a couple of of hours and I don't want you to fall asleep on the job."

"I don't think that'll be possible," she said. Her stomach felt twisted every time she thought about putting Cole in danger. "I don't want to think about that for a little bit."

"I'll take care of it. Turn around," he ordered.

She let go of him and did as he'd commanded. Luca grasped her shoulders and started to massage her. The tension that had had her holding herself stiff relaxed under his touch. He picked up the body wash from the shelf and squirted some on his hands before he started to rub again.

Jade closed her eyes, leaning into him. He began at her shoulders but moved to her neck and down her back. It felt like heaven. She couldn't see him since he was behind her but she didn't worry about what he was going to do. Instead she let him position her arms and legs while he slicked her up. She turned when he requested but kept her head tilted.

"Turn one more time," he said softly.

"Okay." She did so. She felt his hands in her hair.

"I'm going to wash your hair and then we'll rinse you off," he said.

"Sure," she agreed. She was feeling so loosely and limber that she didn't really care what he did.

"Keep your eyes closed," he said.

She let him move her around so that the water washed away all the soap.

"Step aside for a minute."

She cracked her eyes open and watched as he rinsed off his own body. He turned the knobs, shutting off the stream. Jade pushed the curtain out of the way then grabbed one of the towels from the rack and handed it to him.

"Thank you." He smiled at her.

When he looked so loving and kind it made her heart ache. She had never felt as cared about as she did right at that moment. She stepped out of the tub and picked up the extra towel. She started to dry her body but his hands stopped her.

She glanced at him. He took the towel and started to dry her off. He had his wrapped around his waist and his erection tented the material. She hoped they'd be able to take care of that. She'd enjoyed the tenderness in the shower but she wanted his body too.

"Come on." He tugged her out of the bathroom.

She walked towards the bed and spun when she reached it. He was right at her heels and reached for her.

Jade gripped his shoulders as he lowered his mouth down to hers. She opened for him and accepted his tongue.

"I'll make you feel good," he promised.

She nodded.

"Down on the bed," he ordered.

She landed on her back, before scooting up to the pillows. Luca ripped away his towel and followed her up.

"Spread for me," he demanded.

She shivered as she complied. She loved this dominant side of him.

"Good girl," he praised.

It was stupid to be turned on by his words but she couldn't help it. He grabbed a pillow and placed it under her hips. "Touch yourself," he commanded.

She lifted her head to peer down at him.

He nodded. "I want to see you."

"Ooo… Okay." She ran her hands down her stomach until she passed where her trimmed pubic hair started and led to her pussy. With her middle finger she rubbed between her folds. She was already wet and with Luca watching her every move she was aroused beyond belief. She pushed her digit inside, widening her thighs even more. One finger wasn't enough so she added a second.

"That's it, baby," he encouraged.

His words gave her courage to ride her hand. She'd pleasured herself before but never with anyone watching. It felt naughty but exciting.

"I'm going to help," he assured her.

"Please," she begged.

Luca slid one of his fingers in with her two while he lowered his mouth to her clit. He started to tongue her, and she cried out with relief. She was close. Her body trembled and her thighs were shaking hard. Together they pumped in and out while he sucked her.

Jade climaxed, arching and calling out his name. He lifted his head and grinned down at her. "My turn," he told her. He kept his hands clamped on her thighs to hold her open as he scooted forward.

She kept her eyes on him while he gripped his cock and slowly pushed in.

"Yes!" This was much better than her fingers.

Luca pulled out before he slammed back inside. Over and over, until sweat dripped down his face to fall on her breasts. She held onto him and lifted her hips, matching his steady rhythm.

The build-up was slower this time. Since she'd already come once she was able to really enjoy him riding her. She tightened her inner muscles to clamp down on his cock.

"Fuck!" he yelled. He came hard and fast.

He plunged in several more times and she followed him over the edge. Her hands slid down from the sweat on his body. "We're going to need another shower," he said and laughed.

"That was so worth it," she murmured. If he wasn't still on top of her she'd roll and bury her head into the pillow. Maybe a short nap wouldn't hurt.

"Oh, no you don't!" he said.

"What?" she whined.

"No naps," he commanded sternly.

"Fine." She had promised, after all. He pulled out of her, and she sat up. "I guess I should feed you."

"That would be good," he replied. He held out his hand to help her out of bed. She walked to the bedroom door and grabbed the robe off the hook. She wrapped the silk material around her.

"I'll start the coffee first," she told him.

"Even better." He winked before heading towards the bathroom.

* * * *

Jade pulled on her flak vest and tightened the straps. Cole watched her as they stood behind their SUV. He was frowning and she knew that he was still pissed off that she'd insisted on being by his side during the entire assignment. "I'll be fine," she promised him.

"We could have easily split up all the teams so it wouldn't have looked weird for us to be separated," he repeated for what was about the hundredth time.

"I'm not leaving your side," she said. "Jamie will be with us so we'll have another shifter but I'm not taking my eyes off you."

"You could watch from the van," he pointed out.

She'd known that the argument wasn't over when they'd reconvened. It didn't matter, though—she wasn't going to let anything happen to her partner.

"We've been through this," she reminded him. "I'm not going to change my mind."

"I thought maybe Luca would try to talk you out of it," Cole said.

She was a little surprised that Luca hadn't. The only thing he'd said when they'd been on break was that she had better be careful.

"He understands that I have to do this."

"I guess I do, too." He dropped down to sit on the bumper.

She turned and took her place beside him.

"It's just that you are the one person that I can count on. Six months ago I didn't even know you and now I can't imagine not seeing you every day," Cole stated.

"I kind of grow on you, huh?" she teased and bumped his shoulder.

"Sadly yes," he said but grinned at her. "I'll be really pissed off if you get hurt."

"Same goes for you," she replied.

"You both ready?" Jamie asked as he came around from the front. "What's up?" He looked from Cole to her.

"Nothing." She waved her hand. "You just interrupted a really good moment between partners."

Jamie laughed. "Oh, well, no moment is complete without comic relief so it's a good thing I showed up."

Cole shook his head. "How did I end up with you?"

"Just lucky, I guess," Jamie responded.

Both Cole and Jade groaned.

"Calvin's grabbing the keys. I put him in charge of driving so we can go over the map. Jade can ride up front with him and help with directions," Jamie said.

"Patrick's all set on his task?" Jade asked. She still wanted to punch the little weasel but neither Luca nor Cole would let her within five feet of him.

"He's already called in and told them about the scavenger hunt. His boss ordered him to email everyone instructions so they'd know where the teams were going and when," Jamie confirmed. "Since we think they'll hit us before we get to one of the check-ins the van will follow us while each unit will be close to the mark in case we need extra backup. We'll catch them trying to take us out and this will be over," Jamie explained.

"This had better work," she groused.

"Sal and Flynn will be right behind us," Jamie assured her.

"Fine." She glanced at her watch. "We have ten minutes before we're supposed to start."

"Let's load up. You have your weapons?" Jamie asked.

Jade patted the Glock at her side. "Locked and loaded."

Jamie grinned. "I never understood that expression."

She couldn't help but laugh along with him. She had to agree. It didn't matter, though. They were ready to go. She stood and patted Cole's shoulder. "Watch your back."

He nodded. "You too."

She walked to the front of the vehicle and climbed into the passenger seat. Calvin was already behind the wheel pulling on his seatbelt.

"The instructions will be texted to everyone so we all start the game at the same time. Patrick received them early since he's playing the judge and setting up all the boxes we need to retrieve," he explained.

"I'm ready," she said. Jamie and Cole joined them and slammed their doors closed.

"Let's get out of here," Jamie ordered.

"Which way?" Calvin asked.

"Head north for now. At least we'll be on the road when we get the first clue."

Calvin nodded before he started the SUV. He backed out of the parking spot in the Coalition garage. When he reached the exit, Jade glanced around to see if she could spot the van that Sal and Flynn were supposed to be following in. She didn't see them.

"They're watching," Jamie told her.

She sighed and leant back into her seat. She needed to relax.

* * * *

"We're almost at the third location," Calvin mumbled. "Where the hell are these guys?"

Jade wouldn't normally be impatient for something to happen, but her nerves were frayed and she was going to lose her mind if she had to wait any longer.

"Just keep your eyes open. Maybe whoever is after Cole has backed off now that we're involved," Jamie said from the back seat. He didn't sound convinced and Jade wasn't either. The joint task force had given them an opportunity that should have been too good to pass up.

"When we get to the train yard we'll split up," Cole directed.

"No," she snapped. "I'm not leaving you."

"Not far, but look at this." Cole shook out the blueprint of the location. "There are three rows of old metal containers no longer in use. We can go up these and still be close enough to hear if anything happens. But this will also give the illusion that I'm alone."

"We have to do something," Calvin chimed in. "After this we only have one more box to get so that will be their last opening."

Jade turned in her seat to look at Cole. "They might not go for you in the middle of a training exercise at all. Especially with us three here. What if they wait until you really are alone? Shit, they could be waiting at your house now." Crap, why hadn't she thought about that? Just because the other agents had been taken out during operations didn't mean that they would go after Cole the same way.

"We've got it covered," Jamie told her. "Aubrey and her partner are watching his house."

"Really?" Relief flooded her.

"Yeah, we don't know what script these assholes are playing to. We're taking every precaution we can. I keep telling you we won't let anything happen to Cole," Jamie said sternly.

She held up her hands. "I know, I know. I can't help but worry."

"And I appreciate it." Cole patted her shoulder. "But I do know what's after me and I am a big bad wolf."

She snorted. "You've forgotten that you've shifted in front of me."

"What's that mean?"

She reached back and grabbed his ear. She was too quick for him to dodge her. She'd learned quite a bit in the six months they'd been partnered. "I know where to rub to get you docile."

Calvin started to laugh while Jamie slapped his knee. Cole growled but she knew he wasn't really upset. The first time Cole had shifted in front of her during an assignment she hadn't been able to believe her eyes. She'd seen others transform before, but Cole was a huge grey and white wolf. His teeth were long and sharp and if he hadn't been after a suspect who had been shooting at them she wasn't sure she'd have had the nerve to follow him.

There had been a moment when she'd frozen, though.

Once they'd returned to the office he'd informed her that they would spend some time together with him in his wolf form so that she could get used to him. It was during the first month they'd been partnered, and she'd always believed that Cole had been testing her. She'd wanted to gain his trust so she'd agreed.

The next weekend he'd driven out to the mountains and a small clearing that he liked to use. Since shifters didn't need the moon, he was able to transform whenever he wanted.

He'd sat her down on a blanket and told her not to move. She wasn't to approach him when he was in his wolf form. And to only wait for his cues. She could still remember how badly she'd been shaking as she'd watched Cole stroll several yards away. By the time he'd started to strip she had been mesmerised by him getting ready to shift in front of her. And really Cole was an attractive man. It was no hardship to watch him get naked.

His change had appeared smooth. He'd crouched down on his hands and legs. A whirl of wind, a cracking sound that had to have been his bones reshaping, and his skin had seemed to grow. There had been no bright light or a flash, and he was an animal. It was slower than that but quicker than she'd imagined. In just a few short minutes a full-grown male wolf had been in the middle of the grass staring at her. Every movie she'd ever seen had the transformation wrong. Somehow she'd come up with the image of Cole looking half human and half wolf. The thought was ridiculous but she had still been surprised to be looking at an animal that had really just seemed to appear where Cole had once been.

What had shocked her the most had been the fear that wanted to overtake her. She'd shaken even though she'd known she needed to remain calm.

She hated to admit it but every ounce of research had gone out of her head when he'd started to stalk towards her. Yes, she knew not to look him in the eye. To keep her head lower than his. None of that had mattered as he'd got closer.

Without a conscious thought, she'd started to edge backward still on her butt. He'd growled and she'd felt the rumble through her entire body. She had been seconds from running—which she knew not to do but she had been truly scared. Instead of attacking her, Cole had dropped to the ground. Remarkably she had been able to see his eyes and the same look in them as when he was human. A little bit annoyed but calm.

Jade had taken a deep breath and settled back down. With slow, careful movements Cole had crept closer until he'd been at the edge of her space. He'd lifted his massive head, and before she'd known what was happening she'd had a lap full of wolf. She was pretty sure she yelped but Cole was too damn heavy to move so she'd sat there until she'd had the courage to pet him. That was the day she'd learned that he really liked to be rubbed right under his ears.

Realizing that she'd been lost in memories she glanced back at her partner. Cole smirked at her and she wondered if he'd remembered the same thing. If it hadn't been for that bonding experience would they be such great partners now? She didn't know and was glad that she didn't have to worry about it.

She turned back around in her seat to peer out of the windshield. The old train yard's gate was just up ahead.

"Calvin, back up to the fence and stay there. We'll hop over and search for this damn treasure chest. There had better be something good in these heavy ass boxes if I don't get to pound someone into the ground," Jamie bitched.

"I think Luca packed them," Calvin told him.

"Fuck!" Jamie shook his head. "They'll all probably blow up when we hit our final destination."

"I think we're safe," Cole said. "He wouldn't risk Jade."

The three men laughed so Jade flipped her partner off. She actually knew what was inside since she'd been with him when he'd picked up the contents. She wasn't going to ruin the surprise for the others, though.

Calvin moved the SUV in a U-turn before he backed up all the way to the fence and blocked the sign that said 'No Trespassing'.

"Be ready to either take off if we come running or slam through if we call for backup," Jamie ordered.

"Got it," Calvin replied.

"You ready, kids?" Jamie asked, grabbing his gear from the floor.

Jade nodded.

"Let's go!" Jamie ordered.

Jade jumped out of the door to run around to the back of the vehicle. Cole was already jumping over the six foot fence. She sighed, knowing what was coming next.

"Here," Jamie called quietly. He crouched down so that she could climb up his back. Like a monkey, she quickly used him as a tree and got as high as she could before she leapt for the chain metal. She hauled herself over the top and looked down. Cole stood there ready to catch her.

"You'd better not drop me!" she threatened.

He grinned in response. She really wanted to close her eyes but she resisted. Instead she launched herself at her partner. By the time he had her steady on her feet Jamie had landed next to her. Sometimes it sucked to be the only human member of the team.

"Jade, you take the first row. Cole, stay in the middle, and I'll be to your left," Jamie whispered. They nodded acknowledgement before they took off running.

This should work like the first two missions. Somewhere in the middle of all the large trains and mess was a box that they were supposed to capture before any of the other teams. That was the easy part since no one else was searching for their target. The

Coalition and ATF units were somewhere close so that they could reach them quickly if needs be.

Jade pulled out her flashlight and weapon as she reached the front of the aisle she'd been assigned. With the Glock in her right hand just in case, she swung the light around with the left. This location was a good idea for the hunt with all the train cars lined up with plenty of hiding areas.

Lines and rows of old train containers were side by side going farther than she could see with her human eyes. She wasn't even sure if one of the shifters would be able to see to the front of the line. Her shoulders reached the bottom of the train cars, forcing her to swing her torch below and onto the platform that the containers sat on.

She searched one container thoroughly before moving to the next. The moon was almost full so she had a good amount of light with her flashlight as well. Too bad the station didn't have any overhead, though. The shifters wouldn't have a problem with seeing, but she hoped she didn't miss anything.

As she moved to the next container she saw the door halfway open. Well, shit, she really didn't want to go in there. But that would be a good hiding place. She had to set both her weapon and flashlight down to crawl up the side to stand on the platform. The cold metal hurt her hand as she pulled herself up. She was so going to need a shower after this. Maybe she could talk Luca into taking care of her again, since the first time — wow, that had been awesome. She bent to grab her stuff and picked up a soft sound behind her. Staying low, she panned her gaze to the side and farther around her as she turned slowly. She swept her light over the area she'd been in just a minute ago. She couldn't see anything out of the ordinary. No shadows that weren't supposed to be there. Still, she felt freaked out, as though she was being watched. Was someone waiting for her in the container or had she just heard Cole or Jamie making a sound?

She took a deep breath before spinning around in a circle. *No, nothing there.* Carefully, she stepped towards the open door. It was barely wide enough for her to be able to fit through. She holstered her gun and tried to jerk it wider but the rusted metal didn't move.

There probably wasn't enough room for a shifter to get through there, so there was little chance that anyone planned to ambush her from inside. She pointed her flashlight through the opening.

A few old cardboard pieces lay on the ground along with trash and debris. It didn't smell the best, either. She wrinkled her nose. She was not going in there. She started to back up.

She heard the scrape of a shoe on metal. She tried to turn but lost her balance as she was shoved hard into the dark container. Her flashlight rolled away when she hit the ground. Her shoulder ached from where it had banged against the door and it was hard to pull in a breath. *Fuck, that hurt.* She attempted to roll onto her knees but the sharp pain in her back had her crying out instead.

A loud screeching sound alerted her and she looked over to the opening. It was slowly growing smaller. Someone was closing her inside. It had to be a shifter, if the strength of the attack was anything to go by, and now they were able to move the door.

She screamed, but didn't know if anyone would hear. She was sealed inside.

"Ow, ow, ow," she muttered as she very carefully brought her legs under her. She didn't think anything was broken but she would be sore as hell later. Right now her entire body was throbbing. She felt around under her and found the piece of wood her back had hit. She tossed it to the side with all her power and fury. Well, she hadn't seen that coming. She was never going to hear the end of this from Cole. Patting her pockets, she located her phone and pressed the home button. The tiny device barely lit up her hand.

"No!" She didn't have a signal. "Are you kidding me?" she yelled out to no one. "Okay, Jade, use your head. You will figure a way out of this. First find the flashlight."

As she crawled around, searching in the dark, her hands landed on all kinds of trash that she didn't even want to know about. "If there are rats in here I swear to God I'm killing someone," she muttered. She didn't even want to think about what creatures were making their home with her. She shuddered in disgust. *Where's the damn light?*

Chapter Eleven

Luca reached for his water bottle and nearly dropped it when he heard what sounded like a shot. "Was that—?"

"A shot from a high-powered rifle," Zak finished as he yanked open his door.

"Shit!" Luca scrambled to follow him as he jumped out of the driver's side. He heard Abilene and Mitch right behind him as he raced to the edge of the train yard. Luca slid next to Zak when he stopped.

"Check out the roofs," Zak ordered. "There may be a sniper set up. That kind of weapon wouldn't be needed at close quarters."

"Okay," Luca replied as he scanned the area to try to pick up on any movement. There had only been one blast, but if the shooter was trained well enough he only needed one.

"I'll call Jamie," Zak said as he pulled out his cell. After a few seconds he cursed. "It went straight to voicemail. He must have it turned off."

"Jade? Cole?" Luca asked while he concentrated on spotting his prey.

Zak was already dialing, hanging up then dialing again. Luca's stomach cramped as he thought about losing one of his friends or his lover. Who would have thought they'd have a sniper to deal with?

Luca scanned every possible area where the shooter could be hiding. With his superior eyesight thanks to his shifter abilities he should have been able to spot their target. Frustrated, he slammed his hand against his knee. "I can't see anyone," he told Zak.

"I didn't expect you to, but it was worth a try. If we go down there to help we might take fire on ourselves," Zak cautioned.

"And one of them could already be wounded," Luca argued.

"I know." Zak rocked back on his heels. "Okay, Luca and I will go down and check it out. Abilene, you and Mitch keep us in your sights. Try to get a hold of the other teams. See if they heard anything. Calvin, for sure, should have been alerted."

"Be careful." Abilene grabbed their shoulders. "I mean it."

Zak kissed her quickly and they were off, keeping low to the ground to mix their shadows around with the others and to make them smaller targets. They made it to the row closest to them and peered down the aisle. When nothing moved, Zak whistled sharp and fast. The responding sound had Luca taking a long breath in relief. Jamie was okay. Zak motioned for Luca to go first. He plastered himself to the container to his right and darted towards where he suspected Jamie was hiding. Halfway down he spotted Jamie's boot under the wheels. He crouched and grinned at his friend. "Whatcha doing just lying around?" he joked.

"Funny," Jamie replied. "I dropped when I heard the shot but I didn't see anything. Haven't heard anything else either."

"So you're not hit?" Luca checked.

"No, I think it was aimed at Cole. He took the middle passage," Jamie told him.

Luca looked over his shoulder at Zak and held up two fingers. Zak nodded and, faster than Luca could track, started to run. When no more shots were fired, Luca wondered if their sniper had left. Did that mean that he'd completed his mission? God, he couldn't even think like that yet.

"Where's Jade?" Jamie asked as he sat up next to him.

"You were the first one we spotted. Zak is going after Cole now," Luca informed him.

Jamie grabbed his arm. "Let's go. I'm not waiting around here anymore. Did you spot the shooter?"

"No, no sign of him," Luca said.

Jamie growled. "Head straight across and crawl under that wheel." Jamie pointed. "I'll be right behind you."

Luca counted to three then took off. He still didn't hear any more blasts. Maybe the sniper was gone. He rolled when he got to the container across from him before scooting to the other side. From the ground he searched for any sign of Zak or Cole.

There! One car over. He quickly raced to them, hearing Jamie right on his heels. He dropped to his knees and checked Cole over. The wolf shifter was lying under as much cover as he could, covered in dirt and blood. Zak had stripped off his shirt and was holding the cloth to Cole's side.

"He's going to be okay," Zak told them as Luca and Jamie joined him. "It was a clean shot, through and through."

Luca peered at the large cut on Cole's forehead. He had to have hit it when he fell.

"We need an ambulance and backup here now," Zak ordered.

"No! We need to get that fucker. If we call in the rest of the team he might spook and take off," Cole argued.

"He might already be gone," Luca pointed out. "We have to get you help. We'll hold off the ambulance, but get the backup in now. Tell them to use stealth."

Zak nodded.

Cole blinked up at him. "Luca?"

It took Luca a minute to realise that Cole didn't know who was around him. *Damn, the guy must be in pain.* "Yeah, buddy, I'm right here." He patted Cole's uninjured side.

"You have to find Jade!" Cole struggled to lift his head.

"Stay down," Zak demanded. "You'll bleed out."

Cole fell back to the ground but grabbed Luca's hand. "I heard her yell. You have to get to her."

Fuck! Rage boiled inside him at the thought of Jade being hurt. "I will," he promised.

"Back closer to where we came in. The second or third container probably," Cole told him.

"I'm coming with you," Jamie stated. "Remember we don't know if the shooter is still out there so move quickly."

"Yeah," Luca agreed. "Let's go down this row first and then over." He took off without waiting for a response. He would be faster if he shifted into his coyote but he didn't know what condition Jade was in.

When he reached the third empty train car he paused for just a second. He ran towards the first line.

Three quick rounds landed close to his feet and he dove under the container as soon as he was able. He spun to look over his shoulder. Jamie was still stuck in the second row, and now they knew that the shooter was still there. Hopefully one of the other teams could spot him.

He had to find his woman.

* * * *

Jade heard the sounds of three more bullets being fired and cringed. It had been quiet for a good five to ten minutes. Her guess was that one of the other units had arrived and they were being attacked. When she got out of this stupid metal box she was seriously going to hurt someone. The shots had seemed closer but she couldn't be sure. With the darkness around her it was hard to tell what was going on.

She'd finally found her flashlight, but had decided to keep it off for the moment. She knew that someone would find her soon and that she only had to wait, but she could use the big flashlight as a weapon if need be. She didn't want to accidentally shoot the rescue team.

There was a loud thump outside the door. She froze, not knowing if the bad guys were back or if it was her rescue. The whistle that followed, though, she knew was for her.

Since she didn't know if anyone would hear her if she returned the gesture, she picked up the flashlight and slammed it down onto the metal. She did it again and again.

Finally she heard the wrenching scream of the door being opened. As the moonlight filtered in she could see she'd made it to the very back of the container.

"Jade?"

"Luca! Thank God!" she called out to him.

He peered through the opening, running his eyes around searching for her. When they settled on her, his gaze widened. "You okay?"

She wanted to laugh, or cry, maybe scream. Instead she managed a nod.

"I'm coming in," he said.

"No!" she shouted. "There was a shifter out there. That's how I got stuck in here."

Luca turned quickly. He put his back to the opening as he scanned the yard.

"I'll come to you," she said. It would be slow going. Her body was still hurting pretty bad. She didn't want to try to stand without help, but she could crawl. She'd probably been over half the container searching for her flashlight.

"I'm right here," he promised, still keeping watch.

That helped. Knowing that Luca wouldn't leave her and that she was getting out gave her the strength to make her way out. It seemed to take forever and she was shaking and sweating by the time she could put her hand on his leg, but she still smiled. She was getting out.

He angled towards her. "What's wrong? Why can't you stand?"

"I'm okay," she assured him. "I landed on a board, but no permanent damage.

He growled as he reached for her. Gently he lifted her.

"Do you sense anyone?"

He kept her body tight against his. "Not right now, but someone was here," Luca said. "How'd you know it was a shifter?"

"I couldn't move that door. It was rusted open. Only a shifter could have closed it on me," she explained.

"After he threw you onto a board?" he asked.

"More like pushed," she corrected.

Luca growled so he probably didn't really care about the difference.

"Is Cole okay?" she asked. She was afraid of the answer, though, and gripped him tightly.

"Yes," Luca replied.

She grabbed his shoulder. "Luca?"

"He was shot, but he'll be okay. Zak's with him now and Jamie's calling for backup," he told her.

"Where was he — ?"

Luca covered her mouth with his hand and leant farther from the door. Her back protested, but she swallowed her whimper. She didn't know what he'd heard but something had put him on alert. He nodded towards the wall so she pushed off him and grabbed hold of a handrail on the side of the container. He removed his gun as he slowly peeked out again.

"Luca?" Sal called.

Luca put his finger to his lips, telling his brother to be quiet. He holstered his weapon and reached for her again. "This is going to hurt, but I'm going to lift you," he whispered.

"Okay." Not like she had many options. It would be too painful to jump down on her own.

Sal and Flynn were standing guard at the edge with their backs to them. "She okay?" Sal asked when he glanced back and saw Luca carrying Jade. Luca nodded once, but didn't speak.

"Here, pass her to me." Sal held up his arms. "It'll be easier than you trying to climb down with her."

Luca's hand tightened around her for an instant. He clearly didn't want to let her go. Not even to his brother. She was touched, but she wanted off the fucking train car. "It's okay. Sal won't drop me," she joked.

Luca smiled at her before he lowered his lips to hers and kissed her gently.

The handover was pretty easy. Luca placed her in Sal's outstretched arms and she was lowered to the ground. Luca jumped and was right there a moment later. He took her back from his brother. "There are shifters involved," he murmured.

"I can smell them," Sal confirmed. "Jamie's back with Zak and Cole. Cody and his team are shifting and will fly over to spot the sniper. Calvin was knocked out, but, other than a bump on his head, he's okay. He's in the van with Sam and Patrick. The rest of our people are surrounding the place in their shifted forms. No one is going to get out of here. We're just waiting for Cody's signal to begin."

"I need to get Jade to safety," Luca told him.

"I'm fine. As long as I'm not inside that damn eroded box. Just set me down under it," she suggested.

"No, we need to get you away from here. Any one of the shifters will be able to find you if you're too close. Plus we need to get you to the hospital," Luca said.

"I'm fine!"

"He's right," Flynn agreed. "I can take her back to the van."

"I'll go," Luca insisted.

"Flynn knows where it is and can take the same path we did to get back. That way our scent is not all over the place," Sal pointed out.

"Or I can just follow your trail," Luca argued.

"Just give her to Flynn," Sal ordered.

She could feel Luca's body tense up. She leant her head on his shoulder to get his attention. He looked down at her. His features softened. She nodded to let him know that it was okay.

Luca huffed, but, after one quick kiss, he carefully put her in Flynn's hold. Jade smiled for him then Flynn was striding away, taking her with him.

"Is everyone else okay?" she asked when they'd gone out of view. He was making his way over a small hill.

"Yes, we're coordinating our attack now so we'll be able to get Cole out and still capture whoever did this," he told her.

"I can't wait for this to be over," she said.

Flynn chuckled. "I bet. Now what happened to you?"

She explained about being locked inside the container. Flynn continued to stroll along with her as if her weight had no bearing on him at all. When she had finished her story he was frowning.

"What the hell are shifters doing here?" he asked.

"That's what I was wondering," she admitted. "I thought we were up against the agents who wanted to take Cole out, but now we have a sniper and a shifter." She spotted the van and was grateful. Even being carried was putting a strain on her body.

"Well, I guess we'll find out soon," Flynn told her.

The back door of the van opened and Sam ran out.

"Are you okay?" Sam asked when he reached her.

"Yes." She smiled. She really did like the young agent. He might have made some mistakes when it came to his partner, but he was doing everything he could to make up for it.

Flynn strolled to the vehicle and gently put her down on the bench seat. "Ambulance should be around the corner. They are supposed to wait until we call them closer. As far as they know, this is an active crime scene," he explained. "We'll get Cole back here as soon as we can."

"Thanks." She captured his hand. "And you be careful too."

He grinned before turning and jogging back towards his partner and Luca. Jade hated not being involved in the takedown but she knew that she would only be in the way. She looked back at the three occupants with her in the van.

Patrick sat across from her wringing his hands. She still didn't like the guy, but she didn't want to see anyone stressed. "You okay?" she asked him.

"Me?" He jerked back with a look of shock. "You're the one that was hurt. I'm so sorry. I didn't know any of this was going to happen."

She believed him. Patrick might be a coward, but she didn't think he'd had anything to do with the attacks. He was just a pawn, like so many. "It's okay," she told him. "We'll get this figured out and everything will go back to normal." She hoped so anyway. This was more excitement than she had counted on when she and Cole had been assigned to the task force.

The entire mess was pretty unbelievable. Someone at the FBI had lost their mind. To take on the Coalition and the ATF just to take out an agent of their own? Jade couldn't wait to see who took the fall for this. And someone had better be held responsible. It made her sick to think about all the friends she'd made along the way who could now be involved in the plot to take out her partner. Why was being a shifter such a problem? She didn't understand the reasoning. A shifter couldn't help their transformation any more than a human could pick their skin or eye colour. She'd have thought that in this day and time people wouldn't be judged as harshly as they once were. If faced with the same decision she didn't know what she would have chosen to do. She would want to be one of the shifters brave enough to come out but it was easier to say that when she would never have to deal with the consequences.

Could she stand in front of others and take all that hate? She hoped that she would be strong enough but she just wasn't sure. She respected Cole so much more now. She also wondered if he would be able to return to the FBI. Jade wasn't even certain that *she* wanted to anymore. Maybe she should take early retirement and concentrate on lobbying for shifter rights. She'd set out to help people, but now that she knew that her agency was drowning in hate and deceit, she didn't know if she could pretend every day that she enjoyed her job while looking over her shoulder to see who would stab her in the back next.

She knew that a decision didn't have to be made right away and she would talk to Cole about it before she made up her mind, but it was a subject that would have to be brought up.

* * * *

Luca glanced over his shoulder and saw Flynn running back to them. Knowing that Jade was safe would help him concentrate on what he needed to do.

"Everything okay here?" Flynn asked as he joined them.

Luca nodded. "No sign of anyone else."

"Maybe one of us should go under the containers to have a view of the next aisle," Flynn suggested. "The more area we can cover should help."

Sal nodded. "Why don't you do that?"

"Be careful. That is definitely close to being in sight of the sniper. I still don't know where he is, but he almost took me out when I ran from Zak to here."

"Got it," Flynn said before he darted down.

"It's a good thing you weren't shot," Sal muttered. "I would have been really pissed off."

Luca grinned. His brother really did love him. "It's a good thing only you and I went into law enforcement. If you had to be this worried about the others you'd already have a head full of grey hair instead of the few strands you have."

Sal turned his head very slowly and glared at him. "I do not have grey hair. I'm only forty."

"Don't worry," Luca teased. "It makes you look handsome."

"I take it back," Sal grumbled. "Run out there and get your ass shot."

"Oh, come on!" Luca chuckled softly. "It's not that many."

Sal opened his mouth to no doubt threaten him when a loud falcon cry sounded. That was their signal. Luca looked up and saw three different types of bird circling overhead. A shot broke the silence of the night, and Luca finally saw where the sniper was hidden.

Luca and Sal took off down the aisle to where Cody's team had an eye on their target. A loud, long howl of a wolf was next. The teams were all moving.

They raced past four containers, narrowing the distance between them and the sniper's nest, when a black shape dropped down in front of them. Luca skidded to a halt. "Shit!"

A black leopard with gleaming white teeth stood in their way.

"Get down!" Sal called just as the feline launched himself in the air.

Luca dropped to his stomach so that the cat flew past him. Damn, they wouldn't be able to take the shifter in their human forms. "We need to shift," he yelled to his brother.

A roar, one that could only belong to a bear, echoed around them. It looked as though they wouldn't be the only ones to transform.

"You first," Sal ordered. "I'll keep him off you while you shift then you do the same for me."

Luca ran towards the train cars to use them as cover. He slid under and started to tear off his clothes. A shift was quick, but in the few minutes the transformation took he wouldn't be able to protect himself. He started his transformation before he was completely naked. As soon as he was done he darted out straight towards the leopard.

He'd have to watch the cat's teeth, but coyotes were good at working together. He and Sal teamed up could wear down most predators. He just had to stop himself from being bitten while his brother shifted. He circled the big cat, wishing that Zak was there with him too. The leopard was big but nothing compared to the massive size of Zak.

The feline lunged for him but Luca was able to sprint to the side to avoid the paw with long nails that was aimed for his side. He couldn't see his brother and hoped that Sal was almost done with his change. He circled his opponent, looking for an opening.

Sal came jumping out at the leopard, and Luca used the cat's distraction to run behind it and rake his claws down its back. The feline hissed and leapt far enough away from them to show his natural gift. Leopards could also climb damn well, so he and Sal needed to keep him in the open.

A siren and flashing red and blue lights lit up the sky. The leopard looked back, giving Luca the chance to run forward and jump on his back. He sank his canines into his neck and held on with his claws as the feline tried to shake him off. He was relieved when the first Coalition agent in human form appeared. Luca might not be the biggest or baddest of the shifters, but he could do his job. He'd hold on long enough to capture the shifter. But he was damn glad to see backup.

Adam held his dart gun, aimed, and shot the leopard in his side. The cat went crazy. He was trying to bite or scratch his way loosely. Adam reloaded and sent another dart into the leopard.

Tired from the fight and with the drugs starting to take effect, the leopard stumbled. Luca released his teeth just before the leopard collapsed onto the ground.

Adam, Brady and Calvin rushed forward. Sal was at Luca's side, butting his head against his leg. His brother wasn't happy with him jumping the leopard. He dropped down and allowed Sal to rub his snout over him to know that Luca wasn't hurt in any way. The cat hadn't got any marks of his own in before their teammates had shown up. Once Sal was seemingly convinced that Luca wasn't hurt, he allowed Luca to roll over.

Luca strolled over to Adam and leant his weight against the wolf shifter. Adam laughed as he buried his fingers into Luca's scruff and tugged gently. "Yeah, buddy, I'm glad I got here too," Adam said.

Luca opened his mouth to show Adam his sharp teeth.

"Okay, coyote boy," Adam teased. "You could have taken that damn kitty."

He nodded his head, pleased with the acknowledgement.

"Do we really have to carry this damn pussy all the way back to the entrance?" Brady bitched.

"Excuse me?" Calvin snapped.

"Oh shit!" Brady jumped away from Calvin. He'd obviously forgotten that Calvin also belonged to the feline species. Calvin glared at Brady but didn't go after him.

"Yes." Adam pointed between Brady and Calvin.

Brady and Calvin groaned but walked over to pick up the now docile and sleepy leopard. Luca darted in front of them so that he could lead the way and make sure that no one came for them. It sounded as though the fights were over and he was anxious to make sure that everyone had made it out okay. Plus, he really wanted to check on Jade and Cole.

He kept his ears and eyes aware of his surroundings until they reached the fence that someone had busted through. He turned his head as two EMTs following behind Cole as Zak rushed Cole and the bed he was lying on towards the waiting ambulance. Obviously the human EMTs hadn't been moving fast enough for Zak. If Luca had been in human form he would have laughed.

"Hey, coyote!" Jamie called.

Luca turned his head.

"If you want to go to the hospital with Jade, you better shift. They're about to leave."

Shit, he'd forgotten his clothes. He turned to go back and saw Flynn jogging up with his hands full.

"Go ahead and change," Flynn called. "I got them."

Grateful, he moved away from everyone else for privacy. Sal followed him, still in his coyote form also, and stood in front of Luca like a guard until he was panting in the dirt, once again human.

"Thanks, bro," he said as he rose to his feet.

Flynn tossed Luca his pile of clothes. "Go! I got Sal's back."

He pulled his jeans on as fast as he could and was off towards the ambulance as he pulled on his shirt.

"I want to see Cole!"

He heard Jade's sharp, irate voice, and grinned.

"Ma'am, he is going to the same hospital as you are and you shouldn't be walking until we know if your spine was damaged." One of the EMTs was trying to hold Jade down.

"If you call me ma'am one more time I'm going to—"

"Let them do their job," Luca shouted before he jumped in the back next to her.

Her eyes widened. "You okay?" she asked.

"Yes, now be a good patient and maybe I'll give you a kiss."

Jade snorted. "You'll kiss me anyway."

"True," Luca told her with a grin and a wink.

Chapter Twelve

Jade was floating in a haze of pain medicine as the doctor finally left the room. After poking, prodding and X-raying Jade, the medical staff had declared her bruised but okay. She turned her head to watch Luca as he held his cell up to his ear and paced. He was keeping her updated on the three arrests that had been made and Cole's condition.

The Lake Worth Medical Center was one of the best in the country at dealing with both human and shifter patients. Cole had lost a lot of blood but would make a full recovery. Luca noticed her attention on him and stopped beside her bed. "Thanks, Sal," he said into the phone. "I'll let you know when we leave here."

"Everything okay?" she asked when he'd pocketed his cell.

Luca leant over the side of the bed to kiss her forehead. "Yes, the shifters are still sedated. We still don't know who they are, but they're in custody. Their fingerprints are being run to see if they're in any database. We're working a hunch so we started with law enforcement. We should have their names soon."

"Do we need to get back to the office?" she questioned. She could probably make it, maybe, although she couldn't feel her toes. Maybe Luca would carry her again. She'd liked that. His strong arms around her. She'd felt safe and warm. Mmm, yeah, she should have him do that.

She jerked when she felt his lips on hers.

"I don't know what you were thinking about, but I think I like it," he murmured.

"I like you," she blurted out. *Oops*, maybe the good drugs were affecting her more than she'd realised.

"I'm glad to hear it since I don't plan to let you get far," he said. "I'll be keeping you, just so you know."

She smiled. "Promise?"

"Yes. And to answer your question, no we don't have to go into the office. Cody and Sal have it covered. Zak and Jamie are still with Cole so he's not alone. You just rest."

"I'm not tired," she argued. "And I want another kiss."

He peered down at her. "You look like you do right after we make love. All soft, sweet and sleepy."

"Well, if you enjoy it so much," she said, trying to pull him down, "come here."

"I don't think your doctor would appreciate me climbing on top of you after he just looked over every inch of you," Luca teased.

"Doctors are stupid," she whined. She really wanted Luca in the bed with her.

"Maybe, but he also has really good drugs."

"Oh yeah," she agreed. "These are awesome."

"I figured. Why don't you close your eyes for a minute? That way you can see Cole when he's awake."

If Luca refused to cater to her needs, she didn't see the hurt in taking a short nap. "Fine, but don't leave me."

"I'm not going anywhere," he promised. She liked the sound of his voice.

She'd heard some of the others talking and knew that he had shifted earlier. She wished that she could have seen it for herself. Maybe she could talk him into a private show when they got out of the hospital. Which should be any time now. She didn't need to stay. And she wanted to be with the others as they waited for Cole to come round. Plus, she didn't want to miss anything with the investigation. She still wanted to know where the hell the shifters had come from. One leopard, a wolf, and the sniper had transformed into a wolverine when he'd tried to get away.

"Stop thinking." Luca brushed his hand over her hair. She sighed and wiggled her butt deeper into the mattress. She could do that.

* * * *

Luca had brought Jade a pair of his sweatpants with one of his T-shirts to change into for several reasons. The first being that he wanted his scent on her. He was laying claim to her. Second, he enjoyed the sight of her in his clothes. And last, it had been easier to just go his home and grab a shower and clothes for both of them and return.

He helped her pull up the faded cotton pants before hugging her to him. He didn't know how Zak and Abilene were managing to work together when they were so in love. It had about killed him when Jade had been injured. He couldn't imagine what it would feel like when he was deeply in love with her. He knew that's where it was headed. There was no doubt in his mind that they would end up together. He wasn't ready to propose, especially since she wouldn't believe another one so soon, but he did plan to go home with her and never leave. She just didn't need to know that yet.

First, he needed to check on Cole before they met everyone else at the Coalition office.

"You okay?" she asked as she tipped her head back to look up at him.

"Just glad to be getting out of here," he told her.

"Me too," she agreed. "And the doc gave me some of the good stuff just in case."

"Not so stupid now, is he?" he teased.

She snorted. "Would have been better to have you in bed with me, but I guess I'll just have to make sure I get my way tonight."

"Sounds good." He released her to pick up her duffel bag. "Ready?"

"Lead the way." She waved him forward.

"Are you sure you don't want a wheelchair?"

"Yes, Luca." She rolled her eyes. "I'm sore but okay."

He knew he was being somewhat of a mother hen but he couldn't help it. "Just take it slow."

"Yes, dear."

He grabbed her hand as they left her hospital room. Cole had been moved a few doors down earlier. Jade hadn't got to see him and he hadn't thought he could have put her off much longer when the doctor had finally come in and said that they were releasing her. They'd kept her overnight for observation and luckily she'd slept through it. But once she'd woken she'd demanded to see her partner.

He was relieved to be able to finally take her to him. They strolled down the hall until they heard raised voices.

"Uh-oh," Jade commented. "Cole's not happy."

From the sound of things Cole wasn't the only one pissed off.

"You're not going!" Zak shouted.

"You can't keep me here. You're not my boss," Cole yelled back.

"No, but I can keep you away from the Coalition," Zak told him.

"Oh come on," Cole argued. "I just want to find out who tried to kill me."

"You got shot. You need to keep your ass in that bed and recover. We'll take care of the assholes we arrested." Zak lowered his voice. "I get it, man, really, but you need to let us do our job."

"I won't do anything. I just want to be there," Cole promised.

They'd reached the door and Jade peeked inside. Luca was biting his lip to keep from laughing and announcing their presence.

"Just let him come," Jamie spoke up. "I'll make sure he has a nice comfy chair to watch the show from."

Zak growled. "Shut up, Jamie!"

"Maybe we should go in." Jade turned to Luca.

"I don't know, it's kind of entertaining," he told her.

She shook her head before yanking him into the small room. All three men turned towards them as they entered.

"Hey," she greeted her partner, letting go of Luca and rushing over to him. "How are you feeling?"

Cole's expression changed from mad to soft when he looked at Jade. The bond between the two of them was strong, and Luca was happy to be the one to help them reconnect.

"I'm fine. I just wish that asshole would let me do my job."

Zak flipped Cole off but didn't verbally respond.

"Maybe you should stay," Jade told him. "You had to have blood and stitches."

"I don't even hurt. How do you feel, though? I heard you got tossed a pretty good distance last night," Cole said.

"I got the good drugs," she told him happily. "If you're a good boy I might share them."

Cole leant forward and kissed her forehead. "I still want to go into the office."

She sighed before she glanced over at Zak and shrugged.

"Are you serious?" Zak said as he threw his hands up.

"He knows how he feels and we'll keep an eye on him. If someone had shot me I'd want to know who and why. I actually can't wait to meet the guy that locked me in that damn container."

"Fine." Zak pointed at Cole. "But you stay out of the interrogation rooms."

"I will," Cole promised.

"Let's see about getting you released then." Jamie jumped up from where he was sitting.

* * * *

After an hour the five of them were finally walking out of the hospital and climbing into the Coalition SUV. Jamie and Cole were still giving Zak a hard time, and Luca wondered when the tiger shifter would snap. His phone rang as Zak started the vehicle, his brother's name popping up on the screen.

"Hey, Sal."

"How much longer are you going to be?" his brother asked.

"We're headed there now," Luca told him.

"Good."

"What's going on?" Luca asked. Sal sounded shorter than normal.

"We've got a problem with the leopard shifter," Sal said.

"Hang on." Luca pulled the phone away and put it on speaker. "Okay, we can all hear you. What's up?"

"The shifters woke and started to transform back to humans."

Luca glanced up at Jade who was frowning. "Okay, why is that a problem?"

"Sam recognised the leopard."

"Who is it?" Jade questioned. Luca knew that was who she believed had hurt her.

"Sam's ex-partner, Danny."

"What?" everyone chorused.

"Yeah, and it only gets better from there. The other two shifters? All FBI agents and one of them is on our missing persons list."

"What the fuck!" Cole exclaimed. "Why are they trying to kill me?"

"Why aren't you in the hospital?" Sal snapped.

Luca grinned. Leave it to his brother to not only recognise Cole's voice but yell at him for being stupid, too. They all knew that Cole should still be recovering but they hadn't wanted to be the one to tell him.

"Never mind that," Cole replied. "Did you ask them what they were doing?"

"Following orders," Sal told them.

"Whose orders?" Luca asked.

"That's where things get weird. Or weirder. Just get here as soon as you can so we can all try to figure this out." Sal hung up.

Luca glanced around at the others and saw the same shocked expressions that had to be on his face. This was just so strange. They needed answers and they needed them quickly. Whoever had sent Danny and the other two shifters might have already learned that they'd failed. It was only a matter of time before they started to clean house, and Luca was not going to allow them to slip through their fingers. Someone was going to pay for putting Cole and Jade in the hospital. He'd stay on his brother's ass until Sal guaranteed it.

"I don't understand any of this," Jade said quietly.

He gripped her hand. He didn't either. "Doesn't matter, we have them for attacking you and Cole. They'll either talk or go to jail."

"We're missing something, though," she pointed out.

"We'll figure it out," he promised.

* * * *

Jade glared at the man whom she was sure was responsible for her injuries. He kept glancing between her and Luca but wouldn't answer any of their questions. She looked up at the one-way mirror in the room, knowing that Cole was on the other side. So was Sam, for that matter. Maybe they should let the partners talk?

She pulled on Luca's sleeve and motioned to the door. He nodded. Jade smiled at the leopard shifter. He paled slightly, probably wondering what she had planned.

Once they were in the hall, the viewing room door opened and the others stepped out.

"I think Sam should go in," she explained. "It might shake him up a little."

"Me?" Sam shook his head.

"That's a good idea," Zak said as he joined them. "The wolf shifter started talking right away. The wolverine knows he's in trouble — he did shoot an FBI agent. He's already lawyered up."

"No attorney is going to get him out of those charges," Jade said.

"It depends on what they claim. The wolf shifter is John Revelez. We have him listed as missing. But he says he was moved to a new division with the FBI. He was given pictures of Cole and Jade and told that they were selling out undercover agents for profit. He claims he has orders for the job," Zak explained.

"Can he back that up?" Luca asked.

"Cody's heading to the hotel to pick up his stuff. He also gave us the other two's hotel rooms and we have a warrant to get in. We might have enough without them talking, but we really need to get who ordered the hit. John claims the orders were to kill Cole and take Jade to face charges. I don't know what they would have done with you," Zak said, turning to her, "but it wouldn't have been anything good."

Cole and Luca both visibly bristled.

"Has anyone connected the orders to either our boss or Sam's?" Jade asked.

"Not yet," Zak said. "Sal and Flynn are working that angle while we try to get to the bottom of this new department. Commander Green wants us to find out if the other missing agents are in whatever programme they are running."

"Fine," Luca agreed. "Sam and Jade can go interview Danny and see what they can get from him. I'll wait with the wolverine until his lawyer arrives. What's his name, anyway?"

"Eric Nobles," Zak said.

"I… Can I get Danny a ginger ale? He likes them," Sam asked.

"Sure." Jade nodded.

"Would you like anything?"

"Water please," Jade told Sam. She turned to Luca as Sam hurried off. "I don't know what to do with that kid."

Luca nodded. "You'll probably have to guide him through the interrogation, but I think you're right. It will shake Danny up."

"I hope so," she said as she stretched her arms up. She winced slightly, but hoped that Luca didn't catch it. Her muscles were tightening up and she was getting tired.

"You can take a break," Luca told her.

She smiled. "I will if I need to. I promise."

"I'll see you soon. Kick ass." He kissed her quickly.

"You too," she told him. She spotted Sam hurrying back to her. She pushed open the door and motioned for Sam to enter first.

"Sam?"

"Hey, Danny," Sam greeted. "I brought you a drink."

"Thanks, what are you doing here?" Danny questioned.

"Let's talk about that," Jade said as she took the chair directly across from him. She accepted the bottle of water. "Why don't you uncuff one of his hands so he can drink?" she suggested.

Sam hurried around the table to release Danny's right hand.

"I appreciate it," he said.

Jade nodded.

She waited while Sam opened the bottle for Danny and sat beside her. "From what Sam tells me you used to be his partner?"

Danny nodded.

"Were you aware that Sam was there last night with us?" she asked.

Danny's eyes widened. "No!"

"He could easily have been killed or seriously hurt," she pointed out. "You attacked innocent agents, why? You that pissed off at your ex-partner?" she pushed.

"That's not what we were told. You're selling out undercover agents! Sam would never be mixed up with that!" Danny shouted.

"No, I wouldn't," Sam confirmed. "But neither would Jade or Cole. They're good agents. They were going to help me save you."

"Save me?" Danny asked.

"I wanted to make sure you were taken care of. I asked if I could be reassigned as your partner and was told shifters and humans couldn't work together. When I met Cole and Jade and saw they were still partnered, even with him being a shifter and her human, I grew hopeful," Sam explained.

"You said you never wanted to talk to me again," Danny reminded him.

Jade could see the hurt in his eyes.

"I'm an asshole," Sam told him. "I didn't understand and I was scared, but I was wrong."

"You're not just saying that?" Danny questioned.

"No!"

"Use your shifter senses," Jade suggested. "Cole can pick up on feelings and meanings behind people's words. Concentrate on your partner." She purposely reminded him of his connection to Sam.

Danny peered at Sam for several moments before he dropped his head. "I'm so sorry. I was just following orders."

"Tell me about them," Jade urged.

"Right after Sam asked for a new partner, Special Agent in Charge Wilson called me into his office and said no one would partner with me. I could resign from my position or join a new division within the FBI."

"So you took the job?" she asked.

"I thought it would be nice to work among fellow shifters. I had no idea what I was getting into, though," he admitted.

"Why?"

"For the first several weeks all they did was pit us against each other. Had us fight, shift, and show off our gifts. After that they assigned us to teams of three but constantly reminded us that we were easily replaceable. This was my team's first mission."

Jade's heart went out to him. All he'd wanted was to do his job and work along with his fellow agents. The FBI had used him. She was glad that no one had been killed. She wanted to help him. "If I show you some photos can you tell me if they are part of the new division?"

"Sure," he agreed.

"John is already helping us, too," she assured him. "Do you have any copies of anything in your room to help? We already have a warrant, but if you tell us where to look, it'll be faster."

He shrugged. "Everything is in the safe."

"We haven't got anything from the wolverine shifter," she told him.

"Eric?" Danny asked. "We're not close, but he's probably worried about his girlfriend. He's dating one of the other agents—Shannon."

"Shannon?" she repeated. She waved towards the mirror for someone to bring a picture in to her. The door opened soon after and Sal handed her a folder. Jade opened it and passed the picture of the agent she'd discovered missing. "This her?"

Danny bent over the table and nodded. "Yes."

She exchanged a look with Sal. Sal nodded. He moved closer to Danny. "We need you to tell us the names of everyone involved."

Chapter Thirteen

Her body ached and she was dead on her feet but Jade followed Luca into his apartment, ready to be alone with him for a little while. Since his place was closer, they'd decided to head there for a few hours before they met back at the Coalition office with Commander Green. Things were moving quickly now that they had pieced together what was going on with the FBI. After she'd passed the information about Shannon to Luca he'd read Eric Nobles the file on Shannon. He'd been pissed off enough to take back his request for an attorney and had started talking. Since he'd been with the new division the longest, he was able to provide them with even more names. Several agents in charge and even a deputy director.

She was disgusted with her own agency but she didn't want to think about it anymore. Neither she nor Luca spoke as they walked straight to the bedroom. She looked at his mattress and almost wept with joy. She just wanted a few hours' downtime.

"Do you want to take some more pain meds or have a shower?" he asked.

"Bed," she said.

He grinned at her. "Climb in." He walked over to the bed and held open the sheets.

She didn't need to be told again. She stripped out of her clothes before she kissed him and dropped down. It felt so good to be off her feet. She could hear Luca walk around to the other side of the bed before it dipped when he joined her. Jade scooted closer to him to lay her head on his shoulder. He placed a kiss on her forehead.

"I'll set the alarm to give us time to shower and eat," he told her.

She turned her head to lick his nipple. "Maybe some other stuff too."

"That's a plan," he said.

"Do you think we have everything we need to take down the FBI agents involved?" she asked suddenly.

Luca looked down at her. "I do. I spoke to Sal before we left and his boss was already working on suspensions and warrants. He has more power than the players involved. He's the director for the west coast. He has a lot of pull."

"I just hate that they think the shifters are disposable. If I hadn't partnered up with Cole I wonder what would have happened to him."

"Cole is a tough guy and no matter what he was faced with I can't see him getting involved like the others. I hate that it happened to him, but Cole is a leader and he wouldn't have gone along with the type of orders that hurt people."

"You're probably right," she agreed.

"Of course I am. Now go to sleep. I plan on waking you up early enough to make love to you."

She lifted her head to kiss him. "You'd better."

* * * *

Luca groaned when the shrill *beep, beep, beep* of his alarm sounded. It felt as though he'd only just closed his eyes. He was curled around Jade, both of them facing the window. He slid his arm from around her waist to turn over and slap at the clock.

Once the annoying sound had stopped he pulled her back against him. She wiggled even closer and brushed her butt against his erection. He tightened his hold. "Good morning," he said before kissing the back of her neck.

"Yes, it is," she told him. She turned around in his arms.

Luca lowered his mouth to hers and kissed her hungrily. While their tongues twined he cupped her breasts in his hands. He played with her nipples until she rolled over onto her back.

Jade wrapped her legs around him, gripping him tight. "Take me," she demanded.

Luca was already hard and rubbed his cock on her leg.

"Now," she ordered.

He chuckled then reached down and grasped his cock, pumping a few times. He was no longer amused. He positioned himself at her entrance and pushed inside. He filled her slowly.

She arched her back while digging her heels into his ass. He pulled back out in a quick move before he thrust back in.

"God yes," she murmured.

Luca set out at a steady pace. He braced his weight on his knees as he plunged in and out. Jade scratched his back as she held onto him. The bed rocked beneath his powerful thrusts.

"More! Harder!" she cried out.

Luca gripped her hips and raised her up before he started to slam in and out. She was hot and wet. The familiar tingle started at the base of his spine and he knew that he was close.

He lowered his head and kissed her again as she clamped down on him while she climaxed. He shoved himself deep and filled her with his seed.

She held him tight as his breathing started to slow. He lifted his head off her chest to peer at her. "You know I'm not letting you go after this. It doesn't matter to me whether or not you go back to the FBI."

"I don't know what I'm going to do yet but I'll be around," she assured him.

Luca shook his head. "I mean I'll be around all the time."

"Really?" she said. "You planning on moving in?"

He shrugged. "Maybe, but it would have to be at your place. This apartment is too small."

"I knew you would love my house," she said smugly.

"I do. Should we get married first or just live in sin?" he joked.

She pursed her lips. "Well, I'm not going to say yes until I get a ring at least. Down on one knee would probably work better, too."

"So I've been doing it wrong!" he exclaimed. "No wonder you won't say yes."

She laughed. "Yes, that's the problem."

"How about I promise to work on it?"

"I'm agreeable to that. You can start by carrying me to the shower," she suggested.

"You like that, don't you?" he teased. He quite enjoyed it himself so he didn't plan on stopping any time soon.

"Yes!" she told him. "So get to lifting."

He shook his head. "The things I have to do."

* * * *

Cole was standing in the hall when Jade and Luca turned the corner to the conference room where they were supposed to be meeting. She pulled her hand from Luca's and motioned for him to go ahead. Luca and Cole nodded at one another as Luca passed him.

"Looks like the two of you are still getting along pretty well," Cole said.

She nodded and smiled. "You could say that."

"Good." He stuffed his hands in his jeans pockets and shuffled his feet.

"What's going on?" she asked him. She knew her partner pretty well and something was obviously on his mind.

His head snapped up. Jade just lifted an eyebrow and waited. He glanced back and forth from one end of the hall to the other. Even though they were completely alone he grasped her wrist and pulled her into the corner. She went with him, wondering what he wanted to say.

"Commander Green stopped me when I arrived this morning," he told her.

"Okay."

"He asked me if I'd consider transferring here and heading up the wolf shifter division. Instead of using them for backup for the other teams, he would like to utilise them more. Especially now that the FBI is under government investigation," he said.

"That's awesome." She hugged him. "So you'd be heading up an entire unit?"

"If I accept."

"Why wouldn't you? This is a wonderful opportunity. You can still help people and have the support you need. Mitch, Adam and Brady are great."

Cole nodded. "I told him I would only accept on one condition."

"What's that?"

"I won't take the position unless you remain as my partner. I don't want to leave you behind. We make a pretty good team."

Jade blinked at him. "Of course I'm coming. That goes without saying. We're partners."

Cole laughed. "I was worried you wouldn't want to transfer. There aren't a lot of humans working here, although Commander Green assures me there are a few."

Jade waved that off. "I don't care about that. I can still continue my research right?"

"Yes, I made sure he knew how important it is and he even had some ideas about how to expand it to all branches of the government. Maybe even the military."

"So this seems the place to be. But are you sure? You didn't want to leave the FBI before." She had to ask.

"I know." Cole lowered his voice. "But after all this I can't see myself trusting anyone there but you. Even with Sal heading up the investigation into the different offices I'm sure some of the people involved will slip through the cracks. I think it's just too big to narrow down everyone who played a part."

Since Jade shared his concern, she only nodded.

"I want to do this. And we'll get to stay in town and I know how much you love your house."

"You don't have to sell it to me," she said. "I'm on board."

"I had a really good speech planned. I was even going to throw in Luca as a bargaining chip."

Jade hugged Cole again. "I'll let you tell me if you still want."

"No." Cole hugged her back. "Let's go get this meeting started."

She threaded her arm through his and led him to the conference room. She pulled open the door and had everyone's attention. Cole pushed her farther into the room.

"Well?" Jamie asked.

She glanced over her shoulder and saw Cole smile and nod. She was guessing that Cole had already informed everyone, and just this once she would let it go that she wasn't the first one he told. In the future she would make sure that she knew his secrets first, though. That's what partners were for.

"Woo-hoo!" Jamie shouted. He jumped up and hugged Jade then Cole.

She was congratulated by everyone until she was in front of Luca.

"So I've been told that you may be joining us here."

Jade tugged him closer. "That's the rumour. You got a problem with that?"

Luca's grin was wide. "Oh no, I told you before you were stuck with me."

"You're not going to propose again, are you?" she joked.

Luca looked serious for a moment before he laughed. She found herself giggling along.

"I think I'll wait until you meet the rest of my family first."

"That sounds good," she agreed. "Now come here and kiss me."

Luca lowered his head, and she grabbed the back of his neck. She'd never get tired of the feel of his lips on hers.

About the Author

Crissy Smith lives in Texas with her husband, daughter, and three Labrador retrievers. The three dogs love to curl up under her computer desk and nap while she writes. It doesn't leave a lot of room for her but what's a woman to do?

When not writing or reading, she enjoys hunting, camping and shooting. But she has a girly side too and is addicted to pedicures and coffee.

She has been writing since she was a teenager and still loves everything to do with the paranormal. Her stories and characters all have a place in her heart. She loves the Alpha male, the dominant werewolf, and the Master vampire, which find their way in most of her books.

Learn more about the characters she has created at her website where they have their very own page. It will be updated from time to time to let you know what's going on with them. Also you can find out who will be in the next book.

Crissy Smith loves to hear from readers. You can find her contact information, website and author biography at http://www.totallybound.com.

www.ingramcontent.com/pod-product-compliance
Lightning Source LLC
Chambersburg PA
CBHW020729210626
46807CB00016B/794